ENTIRELY

TRANSFORMATION SERIES
BOOK 3

TALYA BLAINE

Ebook ISBN: 978-1-959336-02-0

Paperback ISBN: 978-1-959336-05-1

CONTENTS

STEAMY, SWEATY DUNGEON WINDOW

Conversations at the nearby tables hummed, echoing Quinn's nervous inner buzz. Every so often a cork popped from a pricey wine bottle sheathed in white linen, interrupting the din. Each time a server passed by, plates balanced on forearm, a collage of aromas sharpened into focus and quickly faded away—garlic, a hint of vanilla, coffee, caramelizing sugar.

A waiter approached the table she shared with Leigh and took Leigh's order first. *Thank goodness.* Quinn used the opportunity to sip her sweating glass of ice water, hoping to numb the tight scratch in her throat. Leigh was observant. If she weren't focused on instructing the poor guy on how little butter the chef should use, she would no doubt notice the tremble in Quinn's hand.

Good that Leigh was picky about butter.

By the time it was Quinn's turn to order, she had the glass safely back on the starched white tablecloth.

Montessa was one of Leigh's go-to power-agent spots. Quinn knew she had business to discuss as soon as she read Leigh's text this morning suggesting the location.

But that wasn't why her hands were jittering so damn much.

As the waiter left to put in their orders, Leigh aligned her already-straight silverware and smoothed the unwrinkled cloth just below it with manicured fingertips. "So I got good news Friday afternoon that I wanted to share. Mia not only has that new book coming out—she also was selected for a Hollinger Fellowship."

"Oh, that's wonderful." Mia was one of the authors Leigh represented. An incredibly talented writer, but Quinn still felt a twinge of emotion that had nothing to do with that fact, a feeling a lot like envy.

"It is wonderful. We're thrilled. And since I've been back and forth with the foundation recently, it would be natural to talk to the selection committee about you, to ask how we can get you back there. Even if you don't want to pick up the old novel again"—apparently the silverware had fallen out of perfect alignment and required further minute adjustment—"you could, you know, experiment and start a new one."

Only now did Leigh glance up at Quinn for a response.

"They make such a big deal about it being a once-in-a-lifetime thing. I can't imagine they would make an exception." Truth was, Quinn couldn't imagine going back, the memories haunting.

The whirling red and blue lights reflected in her cabin's bureau mirror.

The sound of the knock at her door.

The words, *There's been an accident.*

The discovery that Harris had been on his way to surprise her after she had hung up on him, irritation and impatience clear in her voice.

Memories she might have begun to learn how to live with but that she never would be freed from.

"If you're open to it, I'll broach the subject. I suspect, for you, they might consider it given what happened. The . . . unprecedented circumstances."

If the unprecedented circumstances hadn't been her own worst, wide-awake, living nightmare, she might once have liked it as a book title.

Leigh could be right. Hollinger might make an exception and let her come back. But there was no way Quinn would *go* back. Someday, perhaps, but not now.

Besides, although she had started to write again, it was not her old novel, and it was not Hollinger material.

She pictured the notebook she had bought in Paris and the pages that fanned apart when she opened the cover from having so many words pressed into the front and back of each leaf. At Hollinger, there would be workshops with the other fellows and readings for the public. Her cheeks heated just thinking about it.

Definitely not Hollinger material.

"I can't," she replied, realization dawning that Leigh wouldn't be gunning for Hollinger if there wasn't still a book that needed to be delivered. Quinn assumed that had been resolved weeks ago. "What did Nely say about the contract when you spoke?"

Leigh reached across the table and placed her hand tentatively on the back of Quinn's. Shows of emotion did not come easily to her; she was really trying to offer support. "What they most want is another book from you, not to fight over the agreement."

"What's to fight about? I said I'd return the advance."

"They could, in theory, claim that's not all you owe, and the amount could be substantial." Leigh waved her hand.

"It's premature to have this conversation—let's not get ahead of ourselves. Keep Hollinger in mind, and if you have a change of heart, I'm confident I can get you in."

The waiter came back with bread from some special flour and a small plate of olive oil. He ground sea salt and pepper over the shiny golden-green pool, dusting it with black and white flecks.

The interruption was a good time to change subjects. "Your text about dinner surprised me—we're in good shape for Saturday, but still—how's the mother of the bride holding up five days out?" Quinn cut two wedges from the crusty, flour-dusted boule and slid them off the wood board onto the bread plates.

"Very well, thanks to all the work you've done. I'm trying to keep normalcy going for as long as possible. My sister flies in Thursday afternoon, but otherwise I'm going about my usual business, trying to stay busy and not hover. It's their thing."

Quinn nodded sympathetically. She saw both sides— Leigh wanting to be close to her daughter in the days leading up to her wedding, and Becca and Charles needing room to breathe.

"I talked to Jonathan this morning," Leigh added. "He sounded so upbeat, despite the job thing. Speaking of, I have *no* idea what he was thinking."

Of course not. Leigh would never understand why he walked away from the network, why he would give up a role like that—the very same question he had struggled with himself. "But I'm delighted you two have become an item."

"We're taking it slowly, but yeah, he's pretty great."

A genuine grin lit Leigh's entire face. There might be distance between the two women, and for more reasons than Leigh realized, but in moments like this Quinn missed their old friendship.

"By the way, you remember Mia's launch party is Thursday, right? You and Jonathan are still planning to come?"

"Yes, of course. I'll remind him." But that twinge of emotion alighted once more at the mention of another author's achievement. It was unwarranted—on top of her talent, Mia was a kind person, and Leigh worked hard to strategize for and promote her authors. Quinn was happy about their success.

Really, she was.

After all, she was the one who had just turned down Leigh's offer to get her back to Hollinger. She was the one who had asked Leigh to get her out of her publishing contract. Both could be hers if she still wanted them.

But she didn't.

She set the last bite of bread on her plate, her mouth suddenly too dry. Maybe she should wait until after the wedding to ask—she had only sent those pages to Leigh yesterday. Leigh was all about inbox zero, but still. There was no way she would have had time to read them yet.

But if Quinn didn't take this unexpected opportunity, she would talk herself out of it. That's why she had sent them off hastily, so she didn't lose her nerve.

"So, have you gotten any promising submissions lately?" she asked.

"The slush pile will bury me alive one day, but every so often something reminds me why I have to read that heap of doo-doo."

Leigh did not say "shit," or any other swear word. "Oh? What's standing out?" Quinn's pulse sped up uncomfortably.

"I read this interesting sample chapter this morning . . ."

Quinn had sent a sample chapter, not only the traditional initial query letter.

"by a debut author . . ."

Quinn had written in her pseudonymous email that she was a debut author. In the erotica genre, that's what she was.

"who wrote some intriguing, promising pages. She has a nice style, and the bones so far are good—"

Quinn let out the breath she had been holding, slow and even, so her immense relief wouldn't be so obvious.

"Let me just say, it's in stark, *stark* contrast to another submission that just came in, which I dragged into the trash folder. I wanted to shower after I read it."

The nervous hum surged, loud. "Oh?"

Maybe she should not have typed up those notebook pages and sent them from a fake address, at least not to Leigh. She did not represent or, as far as Quinn knew, read erotica, no matter how well written it might be.

At least Quinn *thought* her pages had been well written. It was nearly impossible to be a good judge of one's own work. That's exactly why she had wanted to share it; she had been hoping—unrealistically, apparently—for a constructive critique from someone whose professional opinion she respected.

And whose opinion she cared about more than she wanted to acknowledge.

"It was one of those BDSM things." Hard stop, a period not a comma. As if that explanation summed up the problem.

"What was the story about?" It might not be hers; Leigh might be referring to another writer's work.

"Some . . . fancy dungeon in a . . . Parisian château."

Leigh paused between some of the words, with a sarcastic inflection that conveyed obvious disdain.

Quinn's pulse galloped at hearing it was in fact her story. Despite the pounding beat, she tried to keep her voice steady, as well as her hands, which she tucked under her thighs against the seat of the chair. "What didn't you like about it?"

"Well, first—"

Great, she had a list.

"—just what the world needs, more thinly disguised smut. And"—she raised her hands and shook them—"I wanted to scream, 'No, I don't want to join you as you peer into that mansion's steamy, sweaty dungeon window.' I'm not a voyeur, thank you very much."

Peer in the window?

"Are you going to share that feedback?"

"My feedback would come down to two words: Delete. Key. And I probably shouldn't send *that*."

"True," was all Quinn said, concentrating on keeping her expression neutral so it wouldn't give her away.

The waiter brought their meals, and she nodded and mm-hmed as Leigh spoke, occasionally asking a question to keep her talking. Quinn had nothing to add. She would not admit sending the pages, and her embarrassment, her shame, her anger at Leigh's response made small talk impossible. The only reason she was still sitting here was that she had no immediate, plausible excuse to leave in the middle of dinner.

But as soon as their server returned to take their plates, her own hardly touched, she reached for her handbag and fished for her phone, pretending to glance at the time.

"I should get going," she said to Leigh. "The train

schedule is funny tonight. There must be work on the tracks."

"Are you alright? You look . . . troubled. And I monopolized the conversation. Is everything alright?"

Quinn forced a smile. "It's been a long day." Actually, until dinner, it had been a fine day.

"Let's do this again once the wedding is over. It's good for both of us. In the meantime, see you Thursday?"

Quinn caught one of those weird, involuntary laughs before it escaped her mouth. Being around Leigh did not feel good for her, not now.

They hugged goodbye outside the restaurant and headed in opposite directions, a fitting metaphor.

Leigh's comments about the pages Quinn had sent—the start of a short, fictional story inspired by her visit to Madame Manon's estate with Octavia—cut deeply. She was an experienced writer; she knew there was always a risk Leigh, and others, wouldn't like what she created. There had been plenty of times in the past when Leigh wasn't crazy about work Quinn shared with her.

This stung far worse because it meant far more.

It meant starting to write again after Harris. Writing about experiences, questions, desires that revealed themselves to Quinn in ways Leigh did not, and likely would never, understand. It meant taking tottering steps into a lifestyle and community that had helped Quinn get through the darkest, most painful and hopeless time of her life. It meant redefining who she was—as a writer, as a member of Octavia's, and in relation to another man. It meant figuring out how those roles fit together—*if* they fit together—and facing a future much different from the past. Different from the future she had envisioned.

And clearly different from what Leigh envisioned.

Delete. Key.

She should not let Leigh's reaction upset her. She should continue walking straight to Grand Central Terminal and get on that train heading north along the Hudson River. She should go home to her quiet farmhouse, sit herself down at the big old wooden desk in her office, and she should write what wanted to be put on the page.

But that now-familiar need, the need Leigh had so offhandedly disparaged, crested like a tidal wave inside her. She stepped out of the throng of pedestrians and leaned against the wrought iron curlicues of a fence around some chichi apartment building's raised garden bed. The flowers in the cement box signaled the end of the summer, the blossoms wilted, the leaves brown and dry.

She fetched the phone from her bag. Although they had not planned to see each other this evening, she texted Jonathan. She needed him tonight to break the crackling tension and settle her, body and mind.

SHE MUST HAVE WALKED FAST. The elevator door opened to the landing before he finished the draft of the email he'd been working on. He took off his reading glasses and set them on the coffee table, got up from the couch, and went to her.

"Hey, you." After a single slow kiss to her soft, rosy lips, he wrapped his arms around her. "This is a nice surprise."

"I'm glad you were home." She laid her palm on his chest, and he placed a second kiss on the side of her neck and inhaled.

Her hair, as usual, smelled faintly of raspberries. He

would have to be careful at the grocery store; thanks to her, it was now a scent that made him instantly hard.

He pulled back to look at her. A slight furrow knit her brow, and those big brown eyes were hurting. "What's up?"

She hugged him again and leaned the side of her face against him, tilting it up as she spoke. "I did something stupid. It serves me right for thinking it would be a good idea."

"You're one of the smartest people I know. What could you have done that was so stupid?"

"You know those pages I told you I wrote over the weekend?"

"The dirty stuff?"

He felt her cheek curve into a smile against him. "Yeah, the dirty stuff."

He nodded. "What'd you do with it?"

"Well, I put a pen name on it, opened an email account, and sent it to Leigh. I wanted to get unbiased feedback."

Ah. "Didn't go so well?"

"No. Is it that obvious?"

"You're upset, so she must not have gushed about it. Don't get me wrong—I love Leigh, but she has never struck me as the dirty-stories type."

"Right? I told you it was stupid. I knew better. And I did it anyway."

"You wanted feedback, encouragement. She's your agent. She's your friend. It wasn't such a crazy idea. Did she say *anything* constructive?"

"Other than, she wanted to shower after reading it? Or that she didn't want to join the author peering into a steamy, sweaty dungeon window?" She unwrapped her arms from around him and covered her eyes with her hands. "That was pretty much it."

"Ouch. Come here." He took her hands, guided them back around him, and tipped up her chin until she met his eyes. "Her reaction says more about her than you. You're a fantastic writer. I know it was hard to hear those things, but she doesn't get it. What you wrote may be wasted on her, but she's just one person. *One person.* Others will love it."

"It's not that. I know it would find an audience. It's more that she doesn't get it. And not getting it means she really doesn't get me."

He knew there was distance between the two women. Quinn's isolation after Harris died had been so great. Leigh and some of Quinn's other friends genuinely wanted to help —keep her company, take her out, have things be like they used to be. But Quinn, the way she described it, had kept them at arm's length.

Leigh recounted the situation much the same way. He got where Quinn was coming from. The loss was so life-changing, everything else seemed meaningless, and she had little in common with them anymore.

Later, once she started going to Octavia's, he could see how that chasm had only widened rather than narrowed.

"What if you told her? About Octavia's, and about the writing—that it was yours?"

She scoffed, and he saw the dismay in her eyes. "What she said about wanting to shower after reading it—I wouldn't expect much to come out of a conversation like that."

He remembered that night he had dinner at Leigh's, when another writer told Leigh she had heard gossip about Quinn at Octavia's. He still clearly remembered the look on Leigh's face—first shock, promptly followed by disdain.

"Yeah, probably not. I'm sorry." He held the back of her head, kissed her temple with the corner of his mouth. "I wish I could say something to fix it. People change. You're changing. And so friendships, relationships, also have to change. Sometimes the change brings you closer and sometimes . . ."

He trailed off, opting instead to outline her ear with his fingertip, run his thumb down the side of her neck and along her collarbone to the hollow at the base of her throat. "I missed you today," he said rather than finishing his sentence. She didn't need to be reminded of something difficult, something she already knew.

"Come inside," he said while they were still standing on the landing, not that anyone could see them. The entry to the penthouse floor felt wide open to the floors below, but thanks to the creative use of mirrors and privacy glass, no one else could see anything on his level. Kudos to the architect, for whom he felt newfound gratitude—he could in theory take off Quinn's clothes right here.

He wanted nothing more than to make love to her, but he stepped aside to let her pass. "Can I get you a cup of tea?" he asked. "Or wine? Something stronger?"

He took in her shoulders with their slight hunch, reflecting the disheartening conversation she just described with Leigh. The curve and sway of her hips. Her long legs and graceful walk.

She turned to face him, looked up at him with those eyes—wider, deeper brown than usual, suffused with need. "Undress me. Please."

"I can do that." His voice suddenly sounded hoarse. "Come here first." He pulled her close, taking her head in his hands, her dark, silky hair tickling his fingers and making him hard, as if the locks were her fingers on his shaft. "I need to kiss you."

He spoke the words between her parting lips while her

hands found their way underneath his shirt. Her touch made the skin along his sides prickle.

Their lips together, tongues exploring, she took one slow step and then another backward, drawing him down the hall toward his bedroom.

She set her handbag on the floor, and he slid her short trench coat off her shoulders once she straightened. He could smell the restaurant in the fabric as he laid it on his dresser. Walking her back toward the bed, he gently seated her at the edge and knelt in front of her to unfasten the top buttons of her silky blouse, to kiss the crook of her neck and inhale her scent—the familiar fragrance from her hair, the floral and apple notes from her skin.

But it was the restaurant smell that might have been the sexiest undertone of all, for one simple reason: That, after her frustrating dinner with Leigh, after her day was done, she had wanted to come here, to him.

He kissed down her chest, words tumbling out of him as he stretched up and found her lips once again. "God, Quinn, you don't know how much I want to make love to you right now."

Her hand tightened on his forearm, a moment's hesitation that he felt in his gut.

"I need . . ." She closed her eyes and sighed, and he lowered his head to kiss the lids. "What? What do you need?"

"Take over," she whispered. "Take *me* over."

OKAY. So. He knew what she was asking for. Sensation. Pain. To fuck, rather than have gentle, emotive sex like he had been fantasizing about since she texted him earlier.

She had a shitty night with Leigh, and she needed this—to let go, to drown out. How had she put it in the past? To escape. That's why she was here, not because she wanted to cuddle.

He would have to get used to how she needed him, this alternate kind of intimacy. Certainly not less or inferior; perhaps deeper.

But, well, at least for him . . . different.

The memory of the days when he would make the trip out to Long Island, no matter the time, to see her returned. Those days when she would hardly speak, the distant gaze of her heartbroken eyes. It was easier then, when their relationship was one silent, blindfolded encounter to the next, to think of ways to give her what she craved.

Now they were closer; now each touch and gesture, kiss and caress, each entry and thrust and strike held more—a new degree of meaning, emotion, and depth. It wasn't nearly as straightforward.

Since the night of the network's awards ceremony, he had dared to let himself think of what the two of them might become. The rawness, the vulnerability, the openness between them—it was like nothing he had experienced before.

And now that he had a taste, a first hit, he wanted more.

Not tonight, man. What he wanted to give, she did not want to receive; she needed something else.

Redirect. Ad-lib.

It used to happen on the show all the time. A surprising fact, an unexpected comment or a joke from someone he was interviewing, and he would veer off script to capture the authentic moment. At first, it had freaked him out—he never knew in that moment of departure how he would get back on course. But, like a parachute opening mid-air, the diversion freed him to give in, to see what could happen next.

And he always found his way back.

Some of the show's best stuff came about that way, although Mike and Clay might argue otherwise.

Stick to the script, J.J.

Game on; he was done sticking to the script.

"Keep your eyes closed, then. Don't move."

He went to his closet and rifled through the messenger bag, still on the floor where he had set it down after the last time she summoned him to Long Island.

So much had changed since then, and so much remained the same—the undercurrent of sadness that lessened day by day but probably would never fully go away, her craving for release, the way the voice in his head chiseled that question into the inside of his skull: Will you be able to give her what she needs?

The familiar swath of silk grazed the back of his hand. The blindfold.

In his mind, a picture of the last time she wore it took shape—the flush and sheen on her face, her parted lips as she gasped—and the crotch of his jeans grew tight. Yes, the blindfold would be a good start, and he would have faith his mojo would return once things were underway, just like when he had to overcome pre-show jitters before his earliest episodes.

He returned to her, seated on the bed with her eyes closed, her body still but tension evident in the taut ligament at the side of her neck, the way her fingers gripped the sheet beside her leg.

All he had to do was relieve the tension. He had done it for her many times, and he would do it again tonight.

He knelt on the bed behind her and placed the silken

fabric over her eyes. As he began tying the ends, one slipped out of his hand like he was a fumbly adolescent.

The end brushed her arm, and deftly she caught it and raised it to him.

"Don't move," he reminded her, hoping to sound in control, although he felt anything but.

Once he knotted the scarf, he left the bed and faced her so he could adjust it around her eyes. For crap's sake, he had caught a piece of hair. With a finger, he tried to pull it above the blindfold to tuck it behind her ear.

Quickly, quietly, she did it for him.

Shit. He should have brought another scarf from the bag to tie her hands also, but he wasn't going to walk away a second time.

Trailing a finger down the length of her throat and across her collarbone, he bent and kissed the side of her neck, hoping to tease her with sensation and distract himself from wanting to ravish her mouth with deep kisses.

She tilted her head, giving him better access while his fingertips meandered up and down along her neck. The lightest of movements, the hair of a touch, only a few square inches of skin lay before him, vast undiscovered terrain.

She let out a tiny gasp. Good, the intended effect.

So often during his travels he relied on his sense of touch to explore—as he picked up exotic fruits and vegetables in a warren of market stalls, rubbed his thumb and forefinger over colorful, patterned textiles in foreign shops, initially learned about people by the grip of their handshake, the roughness of their palm, the brush of a cheek against his.

He knew how to do this. He would silence the doubts and make the most of this process of discovery.

The fumbly teenage insecurity vanished as he knelt

before her and focused, as he continued to caress her neck
and let his fingers travel, downward over the first few verte-
brae of her back. She leaned forward, the crown of her head
coming to rest against his chest.

If a man could melt, this is how it would feel.

He went back to undoing her blouse, fingering his way
from button to button since her head against him hid them
from view. The thin fabric breezed across the back of his
hands as he slid it off her shoulders, tracing the lace bra
strap along her back before unhooking it and relieving her
of that article of clothing too.

As lightly as he could, he brushed his thumb across her
breast, slowing over her areola, pausing at her nipple.

Her sharp intake of breath encouraged him, and he did
the same to the other. Feather-light touches, a pinching
tweak, gently drawing the hardening nubs into his mouth
and circling them with his tongue, biting the sensitive flesh
—he did all of it, over and over, with only the changes in her
breath, the sudden gasps, the subtle but synchronous movements of her hips as his guides.

In no hurry, he kissed southward along her belly while
his fingertips drew light swirling patterns up and down
the sensitive skin along her sides. He inhaled her scent
and his fingers crept under her lace panties, black and
pretty like the bra, skimming the top of her tight dark
curls.

Okay, maybe he was in a bit of a hurry. But her
breathing hitched, so he inched his fingers toward the V of
her lips while taking one nipple into his mouth and scraping
it with his teeth.

She tipped her pelvis back to make room for his hand at
the same time she found and quickly undid his belt; the
jingle of the buckle as it fell loose sounded to his horny ears

like a winning slot machine in Vegas. This was the thing with her—she awakened every part of him.

Still working her nipple between his lips and teeth, he stopped tracing his path downward and slid his hands around to her ass, moving her from side to side so he could get her panties down her legs and over her feet.

Once they were off, he rasped her nipples with his teeth one more time before removing his mouth from her breasts.

"Hands and knees," he whispered sparingly, guiding her onto all fours.

Playing with her, he slapped, then kissed, then nipped that gorgeous rear end. At his quick bite, she let out a surprised "ouch!"

He spread her feet and knees wider and paused to look at her, her wetness glistening in the moonlight cracking through the bedroom blinds. The city that never sleeps. Seeing her open to him like this, already so wet, he never wanted to sleep again either.

But the damn toy bag remained in the closet. As he sat back on his heels to plan his strategy, the tongue of his belt clinked against the buckle.

Belt.

With a jerk of his wrist, he pulled it through the loops of his jeans. The sound of the worn, supple leather rushing past the denim's fine ribbing got her attention, and she inhaled sharply.

He doubled up the leather, inching the loop from the base of her neck down along her spine so she could sense the strap.

Her breath slowed, anticipating.

He drew the looped strap back and smacked the fleshy part of one ass cheek—hardly with all his might, but not lightly either. And although he was sure she knew it was coming, she still yelped when the leather hit her skin.

She gasped when he did it again, moaned on his third slap, dropped her head and blew out a long breath after several more hard swats in rapid succession.

Not wanting her to bruise or be too sore tomorrow, he soon lightened and slowed his strikes and put the belt down. As he sat back again to look at her, her folds gleaming with dew, he caressed her with one hand while unzipping his fly with the other, stroking himself to the sound of her soft moans.

It was time to lose his jeans.

As he took them off, he told her what to do. "Lower your shoulders to the bed," he ordered.

It still surprised him how his voice changed, how it grew rougher and deeper when he was with her. He had never noticed that with anyone before.

No woman affected him the way she did.

He brought her wrists behind her back and bound them with the belt. His chivalrous side was briefly tempted to ask if that was okay, if she was comfortable, but she had asked him to take over, and that's what he was trying to do.

Besides, she wouldn't be in this position long if the clear drops oozing from the slit of his shaft were any indication.

He held onto her leather-bound wrists and stepped closer, not-so-gently sliding two fingers inside her. Her hip movements, her breathing, her whimpers of pleasure, they synced in time with his motion.

When her muscles tensed and a new release of moisture surfaced, both her tells she was about to climax, he withdrew. "Don't come yet. I want to feel you come while I'm inside you."

The breathless way she said okay, it inspired him to add more. "When I'm fucking you."

It was the first time he spoke to her like that, dirty talk, and he could tell by how her voice caught when she answered, she liked it.

He entered her quickly. With each thrust, he tugged the belt like a rein, occasionally letting one hand go to pull on the scarf's long black silk ties or a handful of her hair in a rough but steady rhythm. And then she cried out. Not words but moans of pleasure, of sudden uncontrollable release that set off his climax while she was still in the throes of her own.

Soon, he unbuckled and unwound the belt from her wrists and removed the blindfold, the usually cool silk warm from her skin. He helped her to the other end of the bed and covered her with the comforter. This was his favorite part, like the gloaming after a busy day and before the dark stillness of sleep, the part of their relationship where she would let him care for her.

He got under the covers beside her and slid his arm around her shoulder. "Thank you," she said, resting her head on his chest, her voice already softening toward slumber.

He kissed the top of her head and closed his eyes. But while his body was ready to doze, his mind was not.

Man, the people she knew from Octavia's would laugh at how vanilla he was with her, how he had fought his impulse to rub her cheeks after each swing of the belt so it wouldn't sting *too* much, the way he had to remind himself again and again that she wanted the sensation—that for her, it was a release.

That for her—with him, and only him—it was sexy and erotic and satisfying.

He thought of his bag in the closet, his trusty bag of tricks. Okay, so tonight he had improvised and added the belt. How long would it be enough?

When she stirred awake a little while later, she kissed his forearm near his elbow. "You get it. You get that part of me."

Hah. If only. "I'm learning." He traced the side of her shoulder with his fingertips. He had watched something blossom in her these last few months. Some aspects might make him uneasy—like her going to the club, although he was coming to grips with that too—but she shouldn't stamp it out, neither in real life nor in her writing. "To be honest, I don't always understand it. But it's beautiful, to watch that part of you unfold."

And then he kissed her, slowly, purposefully, with the expectation she would open to him, and she did.

Since the night of the awards, since that night of love-making, he had started to kiss her without asking, without waiting for her to initiate.

This was how he had wanted to kiss her when she showed up on his doorstep tonight, although she had needed something else. Now, lying in his arms, she caressed the side of his face. Tenderness. This. This—he felt it in her touch—was the start of something unshakable.

NO CHICKENS FOR ME

Quinn was hauling supplies from the house to the barn—strings of tiny lights, thin boughs of curly willow, organza, a *lot* of organza—when Becca texted.

> Impromptu dinner later with your beau
> about the dance. Please come.

She chuckled at the pleading hands emoji, just as a text from Jonathan pinged.

> Heads up: Becca asked me to have dinner
> with her and Leigh tonight. I know more time
> with Leigh is not high on your list, but come
> with? I'll sit strategically between you, and we
> won't stay late. Spend the night at my place?

He was right about having another meal with Leigh. A protective scab had not yet formed on the wound.

But of course she would go for Jonathan and for Becca; she didn't want to say no to the bride, or to spending the night with him. And she could not wait to see his delighted reaction when Becca asked him to have the father-daughter dance.

Becca had decided she and Charles would dance first, and then she wanted Jonathan to join her, while Charles would dance with his mother. "Charles's father and your mom could also join the four of you on the dance floor," Quinn had suggested at one of their meetings, nodding toward Leigh.

Becca's lips had flattened into a line as she shook her head. "I proposed that, but Charles nixed it. He and his dad . . ." She made two fists and rubbed the knuckles together. "He doesn't want his dad involved in the wedding. If it weren't for his mom, I think he would have pushed to elope."

Although Quinn didn't know Charles beyond what Becca relayed, she sympathized with him—it must be hard to live and work in the shadow of such a wealthy, powerful man, especially one whose business reputation and Machiavellian ambition were legend. Now that his father was nearing retirement, Charles would be under incredible pressure to prove he was worthy of taking over the century-old investment firm the men of the Demeleo family had built.

Quinn replied to both texts, and they settled on a small Italian place near Becca's museum and Jonathan's apartment.

Late in the afternoon, after a mountain of wedding things were now neatly organized in the barn and no longer in the living room, she took the train into the city to meet him.

The two of them walked to the restaurant, hand in hand. Despite not looking forward to spending time with

Leigh, for the first time in a long while she felt a sense of ease.

Leigh and Becca were already seated across from one another, each with a glass of white wine on the square table, when she and Jonathan arrived. So much for him inserting himself between her and Leigh—there were only two empty chairs.

"Is Charles joining later?" Jonathan asked as he pulled out Quinn's seat.

"He has to work late. *Again*," Becca said. "Story of our life."

Leigh started to speak, but Becca stopped her. "Right, mom—he's closing major deals so he can inherit the throne. You don't have to remind me."

Jonathan must have sensed a sore subject because he swiftly asked Leigh about the wine.

With perfect timing, a server approached and, by the time he left, the conversation had pivoted to work, and then to their arriving food, and then to the wedding and . . . Quinn's phone rang, the sound set to the shrill ding-a-ling of an old wired telephone. She wanted to be able to hear it earlier, while she traipsed back and forth between the house and the barn.

"Sorry," she said, cringing at the intrusive sound as she rummaged in her bag to silence it.

It rang again before she found it.

"*Someone* wants to talk to you," Leigh said. Quinn's circle had shrunk notably since Harris died, and the people in her life most likely to call her were all sitting right here. Leigh knew that and, Quinn could tell, was curious who it was.

"Apparently." Locating the phone, Quinn peeked at the

screen without lifting it out of her bag. Two missed calls from Octavia.

She took it out, clicked the ringer to vibrate, and began a text message.

At dinner, call you ba

It vibrated in her hand with a third call. A ripple of apprehension moved through her. Octavia wouldn't phone repeatedly like this unless it were serious.

She declined the call and slid her chair back. "Excuse me. I'll just step outside."

There was a crowd milling near the bar. She pushed through and shouldered the front door open. Once outside, she called Octavia back.

Her voice sounded brittle and worried when she answered, nothing like the steady, serene woman Quinn knew. "Oh, thank goodness. Please say you can talk for five minutes."

"I'm here, I can talk. What's the matter?"

"It's Madame. She's sick." Octavia's voice withered. "I need to go to her."

"I'm so sorry." Whatever it was, clearly it wasn't a sniffly cold kind of sick. "Where are you? I'll meet you."

"It's okay—you're busy. But there's something I need to ask."

"Of course, anything."

"I booked the last seat from JFK to Paris tomorrow—"

Quinn interrupted. "Don't worry, I'll drive you to the airport and email the members—you just have to give me the login information for the mail service. And the DMs and I can call everyone right away so they know the club is closed, no problem."

"Actually . . . it's too short notice to close—we have a bunch of events and classes scheduled."

Quinn sensed Octavia hesitating and moved further from the restaurant's door so she could better focus. "I called you because I need you to help me keep the club open. Fill in for me while I'm in Paris?"

Fill in?

"Are you there?"

"I'm here. How long will you be away?"

Octavia inhaled and exhaled slowly. "I'm guessing two weeks. Give or take."

"Two weeks?"

Two weeks?

"I can't do that. I don't have the experience. I'm not trained; I'm not a domina." *I'm not you.* "Besides, I'm always the bottom."

"So was I, Quinn." In Octavia's pause, Quinn pictured her in Paris, taking the lashes of Madame's floggers. "But that's beside the point. You absolutely can do this—the club needs your maturity and good instincts, not technique. Be there to host the events, support the dungeon monitors, answer the phone, pay the bills that come in, that kind of thing."

"I have the wedding this weekend, and . . . For goodness' sake, I can't run a *dungeon*." Quinn's sigh bounced back as static in her ear. This conversation was completely insane.

"It's the worst time I could ask, I know. You don't have to be there *all* the time; the DMs can cover so you can come and go when you need to."

"I don't . . ."

Octavia cut off her waffling. "The club is a second home, a safe space, for many people," she was saying. "It was for you, too. In the last decade we closed unexpectedly only twice. Both of those times were because storms knocked out the power—both happened before we installed the automatic generator."

"Isn't there someone else?" There were so many members and DMs who had more experience than she did. "Alex or Preet or . . . Maximillian?"

"Quinn. You're the one I trust the most to run things like I would, that's why I'm asking. And you can do it with your limits respected. There's no need to scene with anyone; I don't see clients anymore. You'll be in control. Full control. You just have to manage the club as if it were any other business."

"But that's exactly why I can't. I'm. Not. You." At the rise in her voice, several people turned to look at her. She ignored them, stared off into the restaurant window, the glass reflecting layered prisms of light and shadow. It reminded her of the shop window in Paris.

Paris, where she wouldn't have been if it weren't for Octavia. Paris, where Jonathan also had been, peering in a shop window. To a passer-by without the backstory, he would look like a voyeur, to use Leigh's term. But he was not a voyeur; he was looking through the glass because he thought he had glimpsed Quinn. He had been deliberately searching.

When Quinn first visited Octavia's, she too had been searching. When she traveled to Paris at Octavia's invitation, she had been searching.

"I want you to think about something, and if you still say no, I'll close. You have a sixth sense. You knew when to stop Madame; you knew when I needed to stop. Do you remember that night, at the Ball of Fire?"

"Of course I do." What Octavia had needed in that

moment—for the scene to stop, simple as that—had been crystal clear to her.

"And remember how you just showed up at the club your first time, alone? People hardly *ever* do that. They're anxious, embarrassed, uncomfortable. They shield themselves by coming in a group or at least with a friend."

"I *was* anxious and uncomfortable." But it hadn't been so much a conscious decision; she had been drawn there. She had walked in the club's direction, less aware of thoughts or emotions than of the raw feelings—the heaviness, the chill inside her despite the summer heat, the ache. The hope of making those feelings go away, however temporary the reprieve.

She rubbed her chest at the memory, the dull, thudding ache in her soul. How the dripping wax, the sting of leather, had warmed her.

"You showed up. You were shredded inside, but something intrigued you, pulled you, and I dare say you found it. That pull is different for everyone, but the need is there. The members who've met you know you understand, and they trust you."

"Understanding and taking over for you are two very different things."

"It's a lot to ask. But I wouldn't if I weren't fully confident, and if I didn't need the help. The other dominas who sub for me when I go to Paris every year live a plane ride away; we schedule *months* in advance." Her voice shook. "Madame's very important to me. It could be the last time. I need to go."

Tense silence stretched between them, a sparking wire suspended between Octavia's expectation and Quinn's indecision. Octavia was not one to ask for help.

When she spoke again, it was with resignation. "I'm

sorry I put you in a difficult position. I understand if you say no."

Although Octavia would understand, Quinn didn't want to disappoint her. They were friends. The club might be Octavia's professional milieu, but Paris was intensely personal. She had brought Quinn there, let Quinn see an entirely different side of her. And she needed help so she could say goodbye to someone she cared for deeply.

Quinn understood the sorrow of not getting to say goodbye.

Damn it to hell. She rubbed her forehead. "I'll do it."

Octavia sighed with relief. "Thank you. Can you come by the club in the morning to go over everything?"

"Yes, I'll be there."

They ended the call and as she walked toward the restaurant's door, she checked her reflection in the glass pane, as if the decision might have altered her appearance.

———

THE CONVERSATION QUIETED when Quinn got back to the table. Leigh looked at her, expectant. "Everything okay?"

Who was it, and what did they want?

"Yes, fine. It was a . . . neighbor." If she said friend, Leigh would probe. "Apparently, I left the outside lights on all day, and she wanted to make sure I was alright."

The corners of Leigh's mouth lifted into a smile. "How wonderful that they're watching out for you. They must be thrilled beyond belief that you've moved in."

"I'm not sure about that."

"Well I am. You fit right in, the esteemed writer with celebrity friends"—she gestured at Jonathan—"the impeccably refurbished farmhouse and the wedding barn that will, fingers crossed, make *The Times'* Vows section. What's not to love? Just please don't tell me that up there in the country you're going to secretly begin raising chickens or something."

To cover up the snort, Quinn took a sip of the wine Jonathan must have poured while she was out front. "Don't worry, no chickens for me."

Just a latex body suit and Octavia's platform stilettos.

HE CLOSED the taxi door with a tipsy Becca and Leigh tucked inside and knocked on the doorframe to signal the driver. Now, with Quinn's hand in his, he could focus his attention where he had wanted to all evening.

Dessert had been the most distracting. As Becca and Leigh oohed and ahhed over the restaurant's signature chocolate lava cakes, all he could think of was how last time he had made a similar dessert, he had licked droplets of molten chocolate off Quinn's breasts.

It tasted infinitely better that way.

She had been quiet during the rest of the evening; maybe she had been thinking of that night too.

He swung their arms playfully on the walk home, the early autumn air crisp, the leaves on the trees just beginning to turn. Leigh's company tonight must be weighing on her because something was off.

"Hey." He tugged on her hand. "That was nice of your neighbor to check on you."

She nodded, smiled distractedly.

"Did you tell her you wouldn't be home tonight either because"—he pulled her closer while they waited at the corner for the light to change—"I have plans for you; I can't wait to get you out of this." Her jacket was open, and he traced the neckline of her dress, his fingertip caressing her soft skin. "You look very sexy tonight. Mm—" he thought for a moment, "alluring is the word that comes to mind."

She squeezed his hand. "Thanks."

Maybe she was preoccupied with the wedding. "I'm touched Becca asked me about the dance," he offered. "She ever talk to you about her dad?"

When she faced him, it was like she barely registered what he had said. "Becca's dad?"

"Yeah." What was up with her tonight? Going to dinner hadn't thrilled her, but she really withdrew after that neighbor called.

"No, not a word," she replied. "Leigh either—never a mention, or a slip. And after so many years of not sharing, it seems wrong to ask them."

"I know; I've thought the same thing." As they neared his building, Barnes greeted them and held the door so they could enter the lobby. They rounded the corner behind the desk, and he took the key card from his pocket, passing it over the reader by his elevator.

Inside the car, the numbers over the door tinked and one by one turned green as the car rose. She leaned against the wall and closed her eyes.

"Hey." He tipped her chin to get her to look at him. "Is everything okay? You seem distracted or . . . I don't know. Did something upset you?"

Her answer—not exactly the three words he wanted to hear—made his gut clench. "We should talk."

MAYBE THE CALLER who so persistently tried to reach her tonight was a long-lost boyfriend, not a neighbor. "Ohhh-kay. Should I get myself a drink first?"

As they got off the elevator and entered the apartment, they took off their jackets and shoes, left their phones on the kitchen island.

Her smile was nervous as she faced him and rubbed his chest. "You might want one."

Oh, man. "Just tell me." He braced for the "I can't do this" announcement. And no drink was going to help him with that.

"It wasn't my neighbor who called earlier. It was Octavia. Madame Manon, the woman we visited in Paris, is sick. I assume she's dying."

Quinn wasn't sugar-coating it—she had told him how much she hated the euphemisms people used when Harris died. As if not saying the d-word could prevent it from occurring or soften the blow once it had. "Octavia leaves tomorrow to visit her, to say goodbye. She needed someone to manage the club while she's gone."

The breath he was holding forced its way out. It didn't sound like she was dumping him. "And Octavia thinks you have a few substitute dominatrixes in your contact list? Hey, does one of your author-friends moonlight?" He chuckled at his quick humor and took her hand to keep it on his chest.

She cleared her throat. "I guess that author would be me then. She asked me."

Oh.

"And you're entertaining this?"

Her gaze was level with their hands, not his eyes. "I am. I mean, I told her I would do it."

"Whoa. Okay." He let go of her hand. Now she looked at him.

"Jonathan, a good friend asked for help so she can say goodbye to someone important to her."

"I heard that part."

Her eyebrows and lips narrowed; she was getting pissed. "Then what's the problem?"

"Damn it, Quinn. Am I a Neanderthal if I tell you I don't want you playing naked games with strangers at the club? Is that asking too much?"

"I won't be naked, and I won't be playing with anyone. I'm going to manage the club for Octavia for a couple of weeks. It's a job—an administrative job. I can't *not* help her."

He backed away. "I'm going to need time with this."

Maybe he was overreacting, but heat and agitation and images of her at the club were clouding his head. "I think you should . . ." He gestured toward the elevator.

His throat tightened as if a fist were squeezing it at the thought of sending her away, but he could not think this through with her here. He stormed toward the living room in the opposite direction, so he wouldn't have to see her go.

She cut him off. "I am not leaving."

He spun around. She closed the space between them briskly, tugged his shirt loose from his pants, and slid her hands up the sides of his body. Her touch was electric. It always was, and it was no less so now despite his unease, his anger, whatever the hell this cocktail of emotions was.

He took hold of her forearms to stop her, but she resisted. "Let me touch you. Please," she urged.

He softened his hold and her hands moved higher up his sides, then around his back to his shoulder blades. Her fingers fanned wide, like she wanted to gather as much of him as she could.

"Jonathan." She gripped his shoulders from behind, the

pads of her fingers pressing into his skin, bringing him out of his clouded head. "It's a favor. Doing paperwork, greeting people, just being there as the adult in the room. It's a temporary gig. For a couple of weeks, that's it."

He hated this—the incredible pull, the overwhelming desire, and, at the same time, the sinking sensation in his gut at the thought of her so embedded at the club. Temporary or not. Paperwork or not.

He shook his head, brought his hand to her neck, under her hair. Even angry, he needed to touch her. Damn it, the effect she had on him.

His thoughts dissolved like cardboard in the rain. But anyway, thinking would not change anything, that much was clear. The night of the awards, he had promised her he wouldn't ask her not to go to Octavia's. He had promised them both he would figure out a way to accept it.

Well, here's where the rubber, so to speak, met the road.

He could man up or renege. He had told her how beautiful it was to watch this part of her unfold, and it certainly was unfolding now, wasn't it? There wouldn't be a middle ground here—if he wanted to continue their relationship, he would need to accept this.

But he didn't have to like it.

She leaned close to him, and he tried to ignore her breasts against his ribs, her breath on his neck.

"I have an idea," she said, "for us."

What the hell was she going to throw at him next?

"Yeah? What's that?"

"I want to *show* you there's no reason to worry. No one —no one—has taken me where you have. Since we got together, it's been all about me. I want to please *you*."

"You do please me." Her cheek was warm where he

touched it, his insides turning to goo. "Except for your news five minutes ago."

"You're not happy about the club, I get it. But, since I'll be completely in charge there, what if I were completely *not* in charge with you? What if, for these two weeks, I'm your submissive? That's kind of how we started out together, but it was unspoken. That's part of what made it so incredible, but now that we're closer, let's have more of it—more of me pleasing you. More of you taking what you want."

She grinned and tapped his lower lip with her index finger, mischievously. "Consider it an arrangement. An arrangement that makes it more fun for you to accept this crazy thing I agreed to do." She was watching him, her gaze unwavering. "Of course it will be fun for me, too. Please?"

He threaded his fingers through her hair and held her head. "Arrr . . . I don't know what to do with you." He shook his hands, careful not to jar her but still conveying his frustration.

"I'm sure you'll figure that out." Her teasing smile softened the corners of her eyes. Her playfulness was back as she lowered to her knees, his hands still on her head.

His dick figured out what she was up to before his brain did, and it hardened instantly as she undid his belt. One by one, the metal buttons of his fly popped loose from their holes.

He grew even harder as he looked down, watching her maneuver him free of his boxers and . . . *100 . . . 99 . . .* take him into her mouth. Her soft moan made him grab hold of the edge of the counter.

"Quinn." Just looking at her like this—forget the warmth of her mouth or the way her tongue laved and swirled around him or how his balls felt with her hand squeezing them—it practically knocked him off balance.

With his thumbs, he rubbed her head, releasing a small whiff of her shampoo. The smell of berries mingled with her scent as he took in the sight of himself disappearing between and emerging from her lips, as he listened to the suckling sounds she made.

It was a heady concoction—*she* was a heady concoction—but, damn it, she couldn't just do this. Just give him a blow job, even an incredible blow job, and make him okay with her running the club for any amount of time. Did she think he could be bought?

. . . more of me pleasing you, more of you taking what you want.

78 . . . 77 . . . 76 . . .

He was anything but in control at the moment—even with her on her knees, her mouth full with him hitting the back of her throat . . . *65 . . . 64 . . . 63 . . .* his hands tangled in her hair, holding her head in place. Right now, she was the one in charge of the pleasure.

62 . . . 61 . . . 60 . . .

What she just proposed—she was right, it was only a subtle shift from how they had interacted since their first night together. But, for this new quote-unquote arrangement to work, he would have to up his dominance game. Take it to the next level, get creative, push beyond his comfort zone. Hers too. Pick a buzz-phrase, he would have to master it.

Because as much as he loved how they were together, dominance didn't come naturally to him. He would not have told her to drop to her knees and suck him off the moment they walked in the door tonight. For example.

And those restraints he had bought, lined with the soft fleece? They would have to be retired, thrown in the trash.

Later, when she was no longer blowing him, he would order a replacement pair, a serious, professional set.

He looked down at her again.

55 ⋯ 54 ⋯

She had to help Octavia, he got that. He didn't want to limit her in any way—here was this wonderful, strong, sensual woman, discovering a whole new world. It was sexy as shit, and she was asking him to be a part of it with her.

She was offering him what he most wanted: herself.

With her hands, she worked his shaft and played with his balls; with her mouth she alternated sucking him and twirling her tongue around the head.

If there were arguments to be made against being bought, he could not remember them right now.

He thrust faster, grabbed a fistful of her hair, and yanked it. She yelped, and his cock registered the movement of air from her throat.

And then she took him deeper.

Counting was pointless. An algebraic equation wouldn't keep him from coming now.

She swallowed with each of his contractions, and then she licked him clean. His chest heaved with ragged breaths.

She had made a proposal and, he had to admit now, he definitely saw its potential. Besides, she had acknowledged they were a couple, an *us*.

"Stand up." He took her arms and helped her to her feet. "Turn around."

She complied, and he unzipped the back of her dress, slid it off her shoulders and over her hips, held it near the ground so she could step out of it.

Next, he stripped his belt from his jeans while he watched her, amused at how her eyeballs nearly popped out of her head—she would assume that, like last time, he was going to spank her.

"Take off your bra and panties. I accept your proposal. We start now."

———

HE BROUGHT her hands together behind her back and snaked the belt around them several times before buckling it tight and lifting her onto the island. When her ass hit the cold stone, she flinched. Her uncertain look was priceless; he was usually more gentle with her.

Reaching down, he took hold of her feet, lifting them with his palms against the soles. He set them at the edge of the counter, wide enough so he could stand between her legs. His movement forced her back on her elbows, and her eyes grew larger.

She was shiny-wet. His limp member managed to twitch as he parted her folds for closer examination. "Exquisite. And mine. No one at the club gets anywhere near this."

She nodded no profusely.

"Answer me."

"No, of course not, no one. Only you."

He might be too soft to take her, but he had two eager hands and a tongue. The rest of him wasn't done with her yet.

He slid one finger inside her, then two, stroking, prob-ing, stretching. "And no one gets to feel this. No one gets to touch you."

"No one."

"Not even you." He pressed deep, turning his hand slowly so he could rub her swollen bud with his thumb.

"Not without you," she panted.

Rhythmically, he pushed into her and massaged deeper, then lighter, deeper, then lighter. Her head fell back and her moans grew louder.

If he didn't bring her back from the edge, she would slip over. He pulled out abruptly to emphasize his point. "You don't come until I tell you."

She sighed, her hips pitching forward, as if trying to pull him back inside.

"I might just draw up a whole *list* of rules." At that, she uttered something, but it was not a word he recognized.

To settle her, he rubbed her calf, kissed the opposite knee. Ran his hand up the outside of her thigh, her hip, her belly, the center of her chest.

When her breathing slowed, he moved again toward her center, a bee to honey. "I'm going to treat myself to another dessert now," he said. And then he laved slow circles along her folds and around her clit, claiming her with his tongue.

Connected.

As his mouth moved on her, he slid his fingers back inside in one smooth, purposeful movement. Deeper and faster, he bore into her until her cries turned into moans that rose and fell with the drive of his hand.

And then he stopped. He needed to reinforce his rules. Well, so far his only rule, but already he was mulling over more.

She let out an exasperated sigh.

"Your climaxes belong to me, Quinn."

"Okay. Yes," she murmured on an exhale. Her hair was stuck to her forehead. "I was so close."

"Who decides when you come?"

"You do. Only you."

"Good memory." He went back to his work, if you could

call it that, until the sounds she made again told him she was a hair's breadth away.

He moved his mouth away from her just long enough to grant her permission. "Now."

She was there before he finished pronouncing the w. Her muscles held him inside her body, and she shuddered each time he brushed her sweet spot with his thumb.

Once her aftershocks slowed, then stopped, he guided her legs around his waist and carried her to the couch.

She scooted onto her side, and he laid next to her, their legs entangled.

While he stroked her shoulder, she traced lazy circles on his chest with her finger.

"Your so-called arrangement could work out nicely. For us both," he said.

She nodded, her eyes closed, a sated smile on her flushed face. "What changed your mind?"

"It's not changed. I *don't* like the idea of you spending all that time at the club. But I trust you." He kissed her forehead, still warm and damp. He loved that he had made her sweat. "You're fully open and honest with me about this part of your life, so I trust you."

DOMINANT ENOUGH?

Octavia's desk was as neat in person as Quinn remembered from the photos in that magazine feature years ago. Except for the black riding crop placed at an artfully composed angle across the blotter —why had that detail stayed with Quinn all this time?—it could have been the desk of a lawyer or an accountant or any other entrepreneur.

Because it's like any other business. She tapped the keyboard's spacebar, guessing correctly that Octavia had left the computer on. With the username and password on a nearby sticky note, she logged into the calendar app. Today's column still showed Octavia's original departure for tonight, not the morning flight she got onto, standby.

Quinn had been drying her hair at the bathroom mirror while Jonathan made coffee when Octavia called on her way to the airport. "I left notes on my desk. It should all be self-explanatory, but call or text if you have questions. I so appreciate your help, Quinn—it's a tremendous weight off."

Quinn felt every bit of that transferred weight now as

she tried to get herself up to speed, clicking through the well-organized filing system on the hard drive.

It wasn't surprising Octavia was meticulous. The club was her business; the lifestyle, her calling. How, Quinn wondered, had she come to it? She guessed Madame Manon had been a significant influence. Maybe her illness explained the strain Quinn sensed between her and Octavia at the château, the wistful looks Quinn had observed. Maybe Manon knew something was wrong. Maybe she thought she had more time.

A notification pinged on the calendar, refocusing her curiosity from Octavia and Manon's story to the hours ahead.

The cleaning service was due in fifteen minutes. Several members had reservations throughout the day. Open-floor play started at eight o'clock tonight and ran until midnight, with three DMs assigned—everyone confirmed.

Logging into the club's email service, she checked that reminders had gone out to the wider membership. Then she flipped through Octavia's notes, instructions for setting up for tonight on the second page. She would walk the floor to see what she had to do. A dry run, so to speak.

On the main floor, doors to the specialty rooms—fire, fluids, wardrobe, vacuum bed—were propped wide as cleaners flitted in and out, to and from their supply carts. A fold-out "closed for cleaning" sign sat tented outside each, although at least right now, Quinn was the only member here.

The rest of the afternoon kept her busy but not frazzled: Answering phone calls inquiring about membership, talking to the gleeful outreach coordinator who landed a reservation at another recently Michelin-starred restaurant for the

October munch, unpacking boxes shipped overnight. Per Octavia's notes, she put away the contents: chastity belts with electronic timer locks, three sets of spanking paddles in a range of exotic woods, carabiners, satiny black rope, padded wrist cuffs.

At seven fifteen, she changed into a glamorous but modest black lace dress from Octavia's closet and slipped on a pair of black pumps. With the cushy insole and a not-sky-high heel, she should be able to dash around the club for the rest of the night.

A swipe of lipstick from her handbag, three sweeps through her hair with her brush, an extra-deep breath, and once again she headed for the main floor.

The DMs gathered at seven thirty for their routine huddle, and she channeled Octavia as she led the meeting and gave out assignments for the night.

Members began arriving soon after the huddle ended, moving one party at a time from the entry vestibule to the dressing rooms and out onto the main floor, which now hummed with excited chatter.

As she walked around to say hi to people, she spotted the woman from Maximillian's fire scene. She wore a braided leather choker—his collar?—and was about to ascend the staircase.

Level three?

He wasn't far behind, but when he noticed Quinn, he stopped. "Kayla." He used her scene name, and even with his full mask, she made out a smug smile. "I saw the email from Octavia. You've taken over while she's out of town. Inter-esting."

That accent had to be fake.

"Quite brave of you," he added.

Don't engage. She didn't appreciate how he mocked her, but Octavia would take the high road, so she would too.

Her silence worked.

"Well, have a lovely evening," he said after a beat, glancing at his playmate on the stairs.

At ten o'clock, the DMs gathered once more, this time in Octavia's office as usual. It was a perfectly uneventful evening so far, and she said a silent *thank you* that nothing had gone wrong. After the quick check-in, the four of them left the suite together and toured each floor, the club's standard mid-event walkthrough.

The more insight she gained into Octavia's practices, the more Quinn respected her. The club ran like a well-oiled machine, with policies, procedures, checklists, and routines designed to protect the members.

While she returned to the office to check messages and take a break to pee, the DMs continued their rotations. As she passed Octavia's desk on her way out, her phone buzzed with a text.

> COME OVER AFTER WORK. SPEND THE
> NIGHT. (How's that? Dom enough?)

She laughed. All caps. Jonathan relishing his role was cute. And those three words, *spend the night,* sent a warm tingle through her.

She might be tired, but the breeze of a second wind billowed at the thought of seeing him later. Their chemistry was habit-forming.

> Yes, yes, and yes. Very hot. (Shall I call you
> Master? Sir?)

She put the phone on the desk and headed downstairs. A couple of hours later, open play wound down, so she went to the door leading from the main floor into the changing area. As members queued to leave, she said good-bye, just as Octavia often did.

The club's exit process mirrored the entrance procedure, one party at a time to remove a mask or put one's everyday clothes back on. A private transition to life outside the club, another thoughtful Octavia touch.

Maximillian's submissive left alone. When he passed Quinn a short time later, he still wore his black mask. "Goodnight," was all she said.

"Goodnight, Kayla." He turned back toward her. "By the way, when you tire of playing dress-up, sorting Octavia's mail, and standing by the door impersonating a flight attendant from the eighties"—he gave a fake buh-bye wave—"let me know. Life is especially hectic right now and I'm traveling next week, but if you decide to learn about the *actual* lifestyle, let's talk when I return."

NO WAY WOULD he let Quinn call him sir—even playing, that wasn't going to work for him.

> I don't like "Sir."

Master?

Or that. *No.* He thought for a moment.

> Use my name.

Yes, Jonathan.

His dick made an involuntary little hop when he pictured her saying it. Naked.

> Much better.

I'll be able to leave the club soon.

> Text me, and I'll pick you up.

He worried about her leaving by herself so late, and a sudden swell of anger rose as he thought of that fucking asshole who had made her run in fear, her fall sending her to the hospital.

That's alright. I'll order a ride.

Knowing Quinn, she would remember his concerns about pap photos.

> Asserting my D role: Picking You Up.

Okay, okay. I'll meet you outside, at the corner. Thank you, Jonathan.

She added the emoji with the batting eyelashes.

> Text me when you're 15 minutes away from leaving.

The walk would take him ten; he didn't want her waiting out there alone.

I will. But relax. Or I'll have to call you Daddy ;)

> This was your idea, remember?

I do. See you soon. Jonathan.

IN THE ELEVATOR, he leaned back against the railing and crossed his feet and arms, taking her in. She could smell the leather of his jacket. Or maybe it was his belt.

His voice interrupted that train of thought, making her shiver in the best way. "So? How did it go?"

"Well. Surprisingly well for the first night." It was thoughtful of him to wait to ask her, not that she would have shared details while they were walking on the street, where anyone might overhear. The city could be an astoundingly small world.

"Great. You look tired. Hungry?"

"I ran out and got dinner before everyone showed up. I'm not hungry. Maybe a little tired."

"How about a bath, then?"

A warm bath and his soft bed, under the fluffy duvet with him. "That sounds perfect."

He pressed a button on the elevator panel and it came to a halt. "Sounds perfect, what?"

She chuckled. "Jonathan. It sounds perfect, Jonathan." She drew out his name, lowered her voice.

"That's better." His lips formed a mischievous smile. "I like hearing you say it. I could hear your voice earlier when I read it in your text." He leaned closer. "It makes me hard."

She kissed his chest at the notch of warm skin above his shirt button and inhaled his scent, leather and mint.

He cradled her head as he spoke. "Now, when we get to the apartment, you're going to march that sweet ass into the bedroom, take off your clothes, and sit on the bed until I come get you. There's a robe for you hanging behind the door."

"Bossy much?"

"You might have been the boss all day, but you're not the boss now. Are we clear on your orders?"

She liked this side of him. "Yes, we're clear. Jonathan."

His look sent searing heat through her, and the air in the small cabin crackled with desire.

The sudden *zhhhup* of the elevator motor and its upward lurch brought her wandering mind back; she hadn't noticed he restarted it.

Inside the penthouse, she followed his instructions. Straight to his bedroom, changed into the robe, sat on the edge of his bed.

On the edge. That's how he had her. A few minutes ago, she only wanted a hot bath. Now, she was wet. His look, his smell, his smile, his demeanor in the elevator—that's all it took.

She wouldn't like said demeanor in any other man, but with him it was different.

The door from the bedroom to the master bath was closed, but the sound of water streaming told her he had entered through the hallway and was drawing her bath.

Rustling ensued, and soon the door into the bedroom opened and he was coming toward her, naked as the day he was born, his gaze holding hers, his hardness bobbing with each step.

She swallowed as she watched him. Time slowed. He didn't have six-pack abs and he wasn't thirty anymore—hah, neither was she—but he was so handsome. His bright, focused brown eyes and those full lips, dimples when he smiled. Broad shoulders and muscular chest, that trail of curls that ran down his torso . . .

"What are you looking at?" He wore a self-satisfied smile.

"You. I'm admiring."

He paused for a split second before continuing toward her, closer and closer until he stood right in front of her. She raised her hand to touch him, but he took a step back, out of her reach. "Open your robe."

She did.

"Take if off." She slipped her arms out of the sleeves and the thick fabric fell onto the bed. "Turn around and get on your hands and knees."

She did as he asked, wondering if he could see her wetness. But she wondered only briefly because suddenly he slapped her ass. Hard. This . . . her eyes watered . . . this felt like punishment.

"What was *that* for?"

"You said you were admiring me, but I didn't hear my name."

Her right cheek stung. "Jonathan. I was admiring you, Jonathan. I'm sorry I forgot to say it."

"Don't worry, I'll remind you." Her mind flashed to Madame's cane as he slapped her again. Now the left cheek burned equally hot. "Get those sweet, red buns into the tub."

He climbed in after she did and sat behind her, stretching his legs out along either side of her body. Careful in the dim light not to knock over the tea lights he had lined up along the edge, she leaned back against his chest.

Touching him released the tension she had been holding all day. Everything went fine at the club, but she had been on high alert, ready to spring into action if a need arose. "This is perfect, Jonathan. Thank you."

He kissed the top of her head and circled her nipples

with a fingertip. "It will be my pleasure." She glanced upward, one eye popping open at his phrasing. *Will be.* "Do you remember the bath the night you moved into the farm-house?" he asked.

"Of course. Jonathan." That night. He had undressed her, helped her into the tub, and left her alone. It was so considerate and respectful, caring for her while also giving her space. Later, she had kissed him for the first time.

"I so wanted to get in there with you, but I knew you needed to be by yourself. When I left the bathroom, there was this one fantasy I couldn't shake from my brain."

"Oh? And what fantasy was that? Jonathan."

"I'll suspend the name rule while we're in the tub. I want your full attention."

"You have my full attention, and I love saying your name. It's just late, and I'm slow tonight."

"Tub rule suspension in force. And I don't want to hear excuses."

"Okay." She turned her head sideways and kissed his chest with the corner of her mouth. "Tell me the fantasy?"

"I thought of you pleasuring yourself. With a toy. While I watched you."

He laid his forearm across her shoulders and leaned them both forward, reaching with his other arm for the rolled towel at the far end of the wide ledge. He slid it closer and leaned them both back against the porcelain.

"I did some shopping today." He unrolled the towel to reveal four vibrators in a variety of shapes, lengths, girths, and candy colors. "I want to watch you."

"There's a wide selection," she teased. "Which one did you imagine?"

"I didn't get that specific. You can pick."

She selected the turquoise one with the graceful curve,

scooched closer to him, and slowly drew up her knees. With her back against his chest, she could feel him hold his breath as she slid it into her body. It glided easily, despite the water's resistance.

She worked it in and out, reminding herself this was for his pleasure more than her own, so she wouldn't feel so self-conscious.

He kissed her neck, and she shifted against him to move the toy deeper. His erection pressed against her lower back, and his hands reached around and cupped and kneaded her breasts, skimmed and pinched her hardened nipples. His name drifted from her mouth on a moan.

"You know, I think you enjoy being watched." He increased the pressure as he played with her breast and brought his other hand to her clit, circling, teasing. "You remember not to come until I tell you, right?"

"Yes, but—" Instead of finishing the thought, all that came out of her mouth was a gasp. "I'm so close. Jonathan."

Maybe if she said it even though she didn't have to, he would let her come.

He pinched her nipple quick and hard. If he was trying to bring her back from the edge, that would not help—she was ready to tumble over.

He stilled her hand and cupped her chin, holding her to him. "Shhh. Breathe."

Easy for you to say.

He kissed her shoulder, sucked on the bony protrusion like it was her nipple or, *don't think it*, her clit. Slow and sensual.

Right now she both hated and loved how he caught her at the last possible second, dragged her back, made her release all the sweeter.

He let go of her hand. "Why don't you get back to it? I want to see you come."

"Yes. Jonathan." In many ways, he knew her body better than she did, and he tightened his hold around her as she fell.

She drifted toward sleep with her head against his chest, until the gush of warm water near her feet jostled her awake. He was still erect, his hardness pressing against her.

"I'm sorry. What about you?" she asked, reaching back to touch him.

"I'm biding my time. We're not done with you." She felt a tingle, but it didn't have that same igniting effect so soon after coming. He moved her hand back to where it had rested on her thigh. "Pick another toy."

―――――

SHE WAS NOT one of those women who could pull off multiorgasmic feats of superhuman proportion like she sometimes read about in romance novels—it didn't matter how strong her attraction was to him.

The next toy she selected was smaller, with a second stimulator; she would need backup.

He played with her breasts, stroking, tracing, flicking, and touched her while she used the toy. It was as if he were using his fingers to watch.

"Your lips are so full and warm. Imagine me inside you," he whispered after a while, his tool firm against her back.

At hearing his voice, his words, the familiar wave welled and crested, and—"I am . . . I . . . going to come. Sor. . . Jonath—"

"Come for me. Don't be sorry—I'll give you a pass this time."

The sudden wave washed over her; this one had taken her by surprise. He kissed her forehead as she shuddered against him.

"Beautiful." He bent his head to kiss her mouth, nipping her lower lip. "I like our arrangement."

"Me, too."

He tapped her hand, gesturing for her to move it away, and carefully slid the toy from her body. Her muscles tightened around it.

He placed it back on the towel on the ledge and put his arms around her waist.

Her chest rose and fell against him as she recovered. "How do you feel?" he asked.

"Good. Mmm, very good. Jonathan."

"What did I say about my name while we're in here?" He splashed water on her chest, teasing.

"I know. You suspended the rule, but I *want* to say it. And maybe you'll be more lenient next time I forget." She splashed him back, then wriggled side to side to stroke him with her back.

"You shouldn't think about leniency; you should remember to do what I ask you. And I don't recall asking you to splash or tease me."

He splashed her again.

"You're right, Jonathan. I'm sorry." She splashed him back—a move that would be called bratty at the club—then turned to kiss him.

He traced her lips with the tip of his tongue, and she opened to him. He claimed her mouth, and she welcomed his exploration, met his tongue in rhythm. When she brought her hand down and encircled him, his moan—and then his words—heated her mouth.

"I told you we're not done with you. You're not listening

so well tonight." With his index finger, he gently grazed her cheek. "I think you need to be punished again."

She giggled. What was he going to do now, when she was as limp as a soggy washcloth? "You can always punish me, Jonathan."

"You're right. I can." He took her wrists and held them tight with one hand. With the other, he reached into the basket of towels beside the tub and pulled out a bathrobe belt.

He used it to tie her wrists—not terribly tight, but taut enough to tell her he took their play seriously.

He pulled her back so she leaned on his chest again, her hands bound in front of her. Then he reached into the basket once more and lifted out what looked like a remote control. "Are you cold?" he asked.

"No, I'm fine. What are you . . ."

"Shh. Will I have to resort to new measures?" He reached into the basket yet again, sending a big soft towel pluffing to the floor. This time, he held up a red ball gag. "I love hearing your voice, but I'll use it if I have to. Say 'yes' if we understand each other."

"Yes. Jonathan."

He pressed a button on the remote. The drain gurgled, and the water began to recede.

Another press, and warm water cascaded from the tap. When the water level had risen to the middle of her legs, he tapped one of them. "Legs up on the ledge, one on each side."

She did as he asked.

"You sure you're not cold?" he double-checked.

"No, I'm fine." Heat rising off the water enveloped them.

"Then spread wider." He tapped her thighs just above

her knees, then pulled her legs closer in, opening her how he wanted.

He gently parted her folds and placed a toy she hadn't yet used at her entrance. She was still wet with desire, but the bathwater made her skin catch. He repositioned it and pressed it smoothly into her, filling her completely.

He picked up the remote again to direct the shower head down a vertical rail, then adjusted the angle and the spray until a concentrated jet bombarded her most sensitive spot.

She writhed and moved her bound hands as one, trying to touch his wrist. "It's too *much*."

With the press of a button, he stopped the jet. "Shh . . . Relax." He lifted her hair away from the side of her face, kissed the top of her cheekbone, and whispered in her ear. "I read about forced organism today. It intrigued me."

"*Now?*"

"Shh." He put his hand over her mouth. "Gag? Nod your choice."

She moved her head from side to side.

"Lean back. Against me."

With one hand still covering her mouth, his thumb breached her lips, and he rested it on her lower teeth. With his other hand, he pressed the remote and the spray hit her spot-on. He set the controller down, reached under the water, and turned on the toy.

The timed movements massaged her inside while the jet of water beat against her clit. With her legs spread and her calves over the ledge, with his deep dark eyes trained on her, there was no shrinking back, no hiding from any of it.

He kept one hand cupping her jaw, the other her breast, using his forearm as a crossbar to hold her still against him. Her hips bucked against the pulsating stream as the bathwater sloshed around them, the vibrator throbbing inside her until she heard herself scream.

"SO, was that three or four orgasms, Ms. I-only-come-once?" He was drying her off, standing behind her so she could balance against him.

"I lost track." She examined her fingers. "They're as wrinkled as prunes. And my legs feel like jelly."

"Are you sore?"

She paused before she replied, like she was assessing. "Not exactly, but I can tell I had a bit of a workout." Her throaty giggle was adorable.

"Good." He kissed the back of her neck at her hairline, taking in her scent. "Because you're not done yet."

She leaned further against him and sighed. "Jonathan, it's late. I have to get up early and go back to the club."

"Is that your way of safewording?"

She shook her head no. "I'm saying it's late, and I'm really tired."

With his hands on her shoulders, he moved her off his chest, making space between them. He took her hands and brought them behind her to remind her who was in charge. "What did we agree to?"

"I know. I haven't forgotten. I want more of whatever you want to give me."

His balls ached. Miraculously, he hadn't come while playing with her, even as her ass moved against him each time she bucked, each time she came. Especially the last time, her hips pitched wildly even as he held onto her upper body. It was sexy as hell.

"Maybe I want to take." He reached around her body,

caressed her lower belly, and brushed over her swollen bead. He wanted her to take him in; he wanted to drive into her until she screamed his name without thinking—not because of some motorized piece of silicone and the shower spray beating against her, but because *he* was taking her to the height of pleasure himself. He wanted to hear her moan until they free-fell together.

"I'd like that Jonathan."

"That's better. Now, what's your safe word, just in case?"

"I guess it's not the most creative, but how about red?"

"Works for me." He let her hands go and turned her around to face him, securing the towel above her breasts. "Go into the bedroom. Lose the towel. Get under the covers if you're chilly and wait for me. I'm thinking you've had ample foreplay, but make sure you're wet—I don't plan to wait."

He wanted to give her a minute to think about him doing her, so he brushed his teeth. With a hard-on wedged against the counter and Quinn naked in his bed, it wasn't the most thorough job. He should rub one out now and enjoy her for longer—he wouldn't last three strokes inside her like this.

But she was tired and, anyway, he was aiming for more of a psychological effect, of pleasing him even after she'd had enough.

When he opened the bedroom door, she was curled up on her side in bed, her breathing heavy and slow, her body naked like he had told her.

A real dom would wake her up and take her anyway, not think about it twice.

Those old familiar feelings of being a fake, a fraud, of being cast in a role he hadn't earned came roaring back. As he had often felt when he was doing his show, and when he was married to Delphine, he wasn't a real world-traveler, a real performer or, with Delphine, a real good-husband in real-love. In both those huge areas of his life, he was phoning it in, playing one on TV.

Careful not to wake her, he got into bed and under the duvet, cradling his arm around her body.

It was four o'clock when the sound of the faucet woke him, with a hard-on to put others to shame. She came out of the bathroom and shuffled sleepily back to bed. "You okay?" he asked.

"Fine." She got into bed facing him and pulled the duvet over her shoulder. "I can't remember anything after the bath." She was almost slurring, half-asleep. She put her hand on his chest, and he took it and kissed it.

"You fell asleep before your head hit the pillow and I didn't have the heart to wake you. I might need more dominant practice."

Her fingers curled around his hand and she smiled with her eyes closed. "We can work on it. Thanks for letting me sleep. Jonathan."

Her breathing told him she was already dozing off again.

He lay awake staring at the ceiling, the comforter tented with his arousal.

4:10.

4:33.

4:48.

The next time she stirred, he rolled her onto her belly. "You're going to help me practice now," he whispered, moving the duvet out of the way, and touching her swollen, wet lips.

Deliciously, enticingly wet.

He took his pillow and placed it under her hips, brought her hands above her head, and held them together in one of his. With his other, he nudged her legs apart and climbed between them.

"Practice with me, Jonathan," she said, drowsily. As quickly as if his rock-hard tool had its own set of ears, it bobbed in response to her voice, her agreement.

He positioned himself over her and slid into her from behind.

99 . . . 98 . . . 97 . . . He rested his head on her shoulder. "I want this every morning, first thing, before you get out of bed."

"Yes, Jonathan. Yes," she said softly, followed by the sexiest moan he ever heard. 90 . . . 89 . . .

She tightened around him and moved her hips in time with his slow, deep thrusts while he reached around and massaged her.

"And I want you to come when I fuck you this way." He hoped she liked the dirty talk; he certainly did. "Now."

It took a few seconds but soon she cried out, and, damn, the way she rhythmically clenched around him finally released the pressure that had been building in him for hours.

Their aftershocks continued longer than usual, her contracting, him pulsing, the two of them riding the rippling, widening waves.

Like an actual earthquake, this woman possessed the power to rock him, to break him, to cleave him right in two.

WHILE SHE SHOWERED, he made her a cappuccino and left it on the bathroom counter, then hurried back to the kitchen to finish cooking breakfast.

"Hey, have you seen my black skirt?" she called.

The one I took to the seamstress yesterday, so she would have your measurements?

He pictured her in his closet, rifling through the few items she now kept at his place for something else to wear. Since he had sworn to himself he would never lie to her, not even about something silly like this, he didn't answer. She would just assume he hadn't heard her.

"Breakfast's almost ready," he called instead.

"I'm coming."

"How many times have you said *that* in the last twelve hours?" he teased as she came into the kitchen and stood next to him at the stove.

"Very funny. It smells sooo good." She watched him swirl butter around the pan for eggs and lift the crispy bacon from a second pan with his favorite set of tongs. Instead of the disappearing skirt, she was wearing dressy black jeans. "Have you seen—"

He leaned in to distract her with a kiss. She wasn't the type of person to lose track of anything. "Hungry?"

"Starving."

"You worked up an appetite." He set the tongs down and kissed her again, this time lingering to explore her mouth. Mint from the toothpaste, raspberry from her shampoo and conditioner, citrus from her face cream. The mix of scents combined with the memory of how she opened to him last night, and early this morning before the sun had come up, made him hard all over again.

Damn, he could not get enough of her.

She was quiet while she ate, and he tried to contain his grin at watching her enjoy the food he had made her.

This was markedly different from their very first morning together when she was so despondent, he had left a plate for her in her kitchen and hurried home.

They had come a long way. Now she showered at his place, left a few pieces of clothing in his closet and a toothbrush by the sink, and here she was, eating breakfast in his kitchen.

"What's on your agenda today?" She wiped her fingers, shiny from bacon fat, on the napkin in her lap.

"Oh, you know, very important things." Sarcasm helped ease the uncertainty of his employment status.

Or more accurately, unemployment status.

"Actually, I want to work on the treatment for an idea I have for a new show and start researching potential investors so I can produce the pilot episodes." He wanted to do more than that; he wanted to start his own production company and produce pilots for several show ideas, but that was a big stretch, a long shot, and—there were the old naysaying voices again—he didn't want to share his high aims with her.

Because aiming high meant the potential for more spectacular failure.

"That's exciting, a new show."

"Yeah. We'll see. How about your day—final wedding stuff to do? Anything special happening at the club?"

"Wedding stuff is mostly under control—a couple of shipments are being delivered to the house tomorrow but Jerome, the old owner, wants to polish the car, so he said he would sign for them. Which is super-nice. I have calls to make to give final counts, but I can take care of them in between other things, and Becca has her last dress fitting."

She puckered her lips and glanced upward, considering. "I think that's it. At the club, there's nothing special, just a few regular members coming in. I saw reservations on the calendar for the more popular play areas."

"Easier to get time on the big cross thingee and spanking benches on weekday afternoons, huh?"

She shot him an amused but cautionary look, a look that told him part of her still expected him to be a jerk about Octavia's. "Something like that. Don't forget we have Leigh's—Mia's—book launch tonight," she added, possibly to change the subject.

By the way she forced a smile, he could tell Mia's party bothered her.

Why, he wondered. Did she feel envy? Regret? Frustration that she wasn't the one releasing a new book?

He filed the observation away for another time. "It's on my calendar. Come here first, and we'll go over together. And plan to spend the night."

She met his gaze with those beautiful eyes. "I will. Jonathan."

He could get used to this. As she brought their plates to the sink, he watched how her long back and silky hair moved with each step. Somehow, that image morphed to one of her on her knees, sucking him off.

She set the plates down and turned back toward him, as if she felt his stare. "What? What's that look?"

"Nothing. I just had a thought."

"About?"

"Get to the club, or I'll keep you here all day." He stood and took her by the forearms, brought her close so he could kiss her goodbye.

Instead, she undid his button and fly and floated down to her knees as she freed him from his jeans and boxers.

Had his fantasy drifted outside his head and appeared in a thought balloon, or was it the growing bulge in his pants that had given him away?

With a stroke of her index finger, she wiped the clear drops from the tip of his shaft, sucked them off her skin, and looked up at him. "Oh, I don't think this will take all day."

FLUSHED

On Thursday, Alex and the rest of the evening DMs arrived at five o'clock. Quinn briefed them during a quick huddle before jogging up to Octavia's suite to change back into her jeans and sneakers. During rush hour, walking to Jonathan's would be the quickest way.

Not that she was in a great hurry to get to Leigh's launch party for Mia.

His elevator whisked her up to the penthouse and as she headed inside, Jonathan emerged from the bedroom, a towel wrapped sexily around his hips. She stood on tiptoes to kiss him hello. "I didn't hear it," he murmured, their lips still touching.

"It's a really quiet elevator."

He pulled away and gaped. "I wasn't talking about the elevator."

Shit. "Jonathan. I'm sorry, Jonathan." Again, she kissed him, putting one hand on his side, gently tickling with her nails. "Jonathan, hi," she whispered. "Is that better?"

"That's better. I'm not saying you won't be punished this evening for forgetting, but that was definitely better."

"Okay, good," she teased.

"I guess your punishments haven't been severe enough if it's funny."

"Your punishments, Jonathan, have been . . . wonderful. I wasn't making light of them." Her mind went to Madame's cane in Paris. She could bring one home from the club for him—for both of them.

"Get in the shower. We have to leave soon."

"Yes, Jonathan."

When she came out of the bathroom, the black silk cocktail dress she had left hanging on the closet door for tonight was gone. In its place hung a slinky black jumpsuit with a deep halter neck and wide flowy legs. The top half was more revealing than she would ever wear—bare shoulders, an open back, cleavage. This sailed way beyond her modesty comfort zone. But it was gorgeous.

"Is this what you'd like me to wear tonight, Jonathan?" It looked like it would fit, but she checked for a label with the size. There wasn't one. Did he have it custom made?

He sat on the edge of the bed watching her, heat and hunger in his eyes. "It is. And do not even think about wearing panties."

———

LEIGH WAS GREETING guests by the entrance to the party space, a swanky loft and rooftop terrace. While Quinn and Jonathan waited to say hi, his hand found the small of her back beneath the soft black cashmere cape he gave her as they left his apartment.

The couple ahead of them proceeded to the spiral metal

staircase, and Leigh hugged her and, next, Jonathan, then stood back to give Quinn the once over. "You look striking. That outfit is"—her eyes traveled down and up Quinn's body—"quite dramatic."

They headed up to the open loft, with its high ceilings, exposed ductwork, and brick walls. A crowd was gathered around Mia, and Quinn reached for Jonathan's hand. It wasn't that she missed being the center of attention—she had never liked that. No, it was more that the part of her that once had a successful career as a respected author had fallen away. And that felt strange, unnerving, another loss all its own.

Leigh's comments about the anonymous work she had sent echoed in her mind.

Distasteful. Smut. Voyeur.

Jonathan squeezed her hand. Without her saying anything, he knew what she was thinking.

"You can do it, too," he said. "If you want to, you can write another brilliant book. Nothing's changed. If anything, you have more experience in you to write about than before. If that's what you want, I'll help you however I can—you know that, right?"

She gripped his hand, threaded her other one around his arm, and leaned into him, a sideways hug. "I do." He was her steadfast supporter, one of the many qualities that made her fall, each day, a little deeper.

A little deeper . . . Why was it so hard to complete that thought?

Fortunately, she didn't have to. "So where to? Should we mingle?" he asked, planting a kiss at the top of her head.

"Yes, let's." Her introverted self usually shuddered at the word, but she wanted to congratulate Mia and say hello to the other writer-acquaintances she spotted on the way in, her own toned-down version of mingling. Plus, with him beside her, it would be easier. He made a lot of things easier.

She rubbed his bicep, and together they headed toward Mia to join the circle around her.

A little later, during a lull in the conversation, the group dissipated. "How about some air?" he asked. His hand returned to her lower back, and he guided her to an opening in the wall of floor-to-ceiling glass panes and onto the wrap-around terrace. Tall heaters, much like the ones she rented for the barn on Saturday, warmed the cool twilight air.

They wove among the islands of people to a spot along the glass balustrade. An adjacent skyscraper cast a fading shadow over guests talking nearby, wineglasses in their hands.

Facing each other, he brushed the back of his fingers over her cheek, looked at her hair, her face, her neck. "How are you doing?"

"Okay. It's just, I keep hearing what Leigh said about those pages being smut." She leaned her forehead against him, shaking it.

"Hey." He stilled her head. "Look at me." She met his eyes, caring and magnetic. "Don't think about that now. You do you. You're . . ."

He was reaching for the right words. "Quinn, you're like this delicate flower bud that's turning toward the sun and just starting to open. Cheesy analogy maybe, but that's how I see you. Just starting to open." His voice dropped to a whisper.

He stroked her cheek again, this time with the pads of his fingers, warm and tender. "See where it takes you." At that, she met his lips with hers; he was beginning to taste familiar.

Delicious and familiar.

He held her against him a moment, then leaned down and whispered in her ear, his voice different now. Lower, rougher. Hotter.

"I want you to open up." He kissed her again, biting her lower lip. She knew what he meant; she wanted it too.

"We've made an appearance," she said, reaching under his sport coat to rub his side. "Let's go home."

"No." His voice was gruff. "Here."

He turned her so she faced the city, with its lights and horns and sirens, the high floors of the buildings around them chessboards of dark and light. "Yes," he added, "I think right here is perfect."

He stood behind her, only thin layers of fabric between his body and her skin. She felt his hand near her hip, by the pocket of the jumpsuit. He slid it in and . . . She gasped at his touch and grabbed his wrist. "Stop it!" she hissed. "People will see."

It's a good thing she hadn't put anything valuable in that pocket. Although that wasn't the right word, since *pocket* implied a space that was closed on three sides. This was—he spread her lips, already wet, and circled her bead with his finger—definitely not a pocket. "*Jonathan.* What are you *doing?*"

"Hands on the railing. Both of them." He swatted her lips with his straightened fingers, sending a current straight through her.

From most vantage points on the terrace, they would— she really, really hoped—look like any affectionate couple, a man standing behind a woman to keep her warm, to shield her from the breeze as they looked out together at the Manhattan skyline.

His hardness pressed against the small of her back, and his body held her between him and the thick glass panel. Snippets of conversation darted around them, wrapped in scents of aftershave and perfume as the other guests moved about. High heels click-clacked while men's loafers tapped against the tile. She prayed none of the people standing on either side of them would glance left or right.

Now he was sliding the side of his finger back and forth along her lips, which seemed to have reached a new level of sensitivity.

"Would you *stop*?" She grabbed his wrist again. "Please stop."

"Safe word or silence, and put your hand back on the railing." He paused his motion, and she took a deep breath.

But now he was back to rubbing small circles around her clit, alternating with hard, direct pressure. It throbbed like a beating heart.

His cock rustled against her back as he slid one, then two fingers inside her. "Not here, Jonathan. Someone will see."

"Then you better get off fast." His breath against her ear sent chills downward while heat rose from her core, a dance of sensation.

He nudged the hair away from her ear to get closer. "Do you want them to see the look on your face when you come, or see my wet fingers coming out of your pants?"

She swallowed the moan rising fast in her throat to stay quiet. This was a side of him he had not shown her before.

She liked it, she had to admit. Very much.

He was sliding his fingers along the length of her again —back and forth, back and forth, returning again and again to circle her clit.

"You are so wet," he whispered. "Who are you wet for? Because there are so many people around us—I'm not sure."

Without looking at his face, she could picture his teasing smile.

"You, Jonathan, you," she managed to get out.

"Show me it's me." His words. His breath on the rim of her ear. His voice barely a murmur. His rhythm increasing, fingers stroking with each thrust. "Come for me."

It wasn't long before the white lights on the neighboring buildings flashed and her eyes squeezed shut. His body closed protectively in around her, and she grasped the ledge tighter, although in a way she had already fallen over it.

Voices rose next to them. People were moving. He shifted his body to block her from view and pecked the top of her head as she clenched around him, her breathing hard and heavy.

Once she was still, he removed his hand from the faux pocket, repositioned the fabric, and held her close. "That was incredibly sexy."

She tipped her head back to tap his chest. "I do not believe you just did that. *Here,* of all places."

"And you will be punished later for resisting." His smile was evil, although he took off his sport coat and wrapped it around her shoulders, over the cape.

"*There* you are." Leigh appeared behind them, giving each of their backs a quick rub. "I was wondering where you two scurried off to."

Quinn turned toward her, grateful the twilight had softened to darkness since they had come outside.

"I'm so happy you're here," Leigh said. Quinn had declined who knew how many of these events in the surreal span of time since Harris died.

Jonathan jumped in to redirect. "How is the mother of the bride? We're getting down to T-minus territory." Quinn gave his hand a thank-you squeeze.

"Glad to have this to focus on," Leigh answered. "I was asked not to hover; I'm not hovering." She turned her arm to check her smartwatch. "Becca's at her fitting right now, and I have refrained from texting to request a photo."

Jonathan laughed. "Impressive restraint."

"I started reading Mia's book," Quinn offered. "The writing is fabulous."

Leigh nodded, agreeing. "She's good. Like you. I wish *you* would write again so I could throw a party like this to celebrate . . . a fresh start—" She touched Quinn's arm. "I know, I've heard what you've said, I have. But what do you think about playing with some new ideas, just, you know, for fun? Show me a few pages?"

I already did.

Quinn forced a smile. "I'll try." Jonathan reached for her hand just as Leigh glanced at the red-wine glass someone had abandoned on the ledge nearby. Quinn's face heated at seeing it, a reminder of just how close other guests had stood.

Leigh lifted her gaze from the glass, partly full, red lipstick on the rim, and turned back toward Quinn. "You're flushed—how's the wine?"

SHE STAYED TUCKED against Jonathan the entire ride home, his arm draped around her shoulders. He wanted to ask her if tonight had been okay, if she liked it, to tell her not to worry, that he would never let anyone see her exposed.

But he also knew that fear and risk, although the situation was controlled, heightened the effect. Reassuring her too much might dull the razor-thin edge they played on; it might take the thrill away.

Most thrilling to him were the trust and affection growing between them. Little by little, she was moving closer. She might go to the club to manage day-to-day stuff for Octavia, but that was all; to play, she came home to him.

He got back into character and gently brought her head toward him. "You still have a punishment coming at some point, remember?"

"I remember, Jonathan." She surprised him with a kiss, a simple peck high on his arm. "What kind of punishment?" She sounded mellow and groggy, sated, but—he loved this facet of her personality—playful.

"That's for me to know and you to find out."

That's for me to figure out.

"Please, just promise me you won't do what you did tonight on Saturday." She shook her head from side to side against his arm. "I cannot believe you."

He chuckled and rubbed her arm. "I think you liked it."

"I might have. But my heart was pounding the whole time—if someone saw, I would have been mortified."

"I think risking that possibility for an intense orgasm —*in a crowded place*—is the point." He couldn't resist reminding her. And he would definitely have to up his dominance game while they had their little arrangement in place. It was proving good for their relationship. "Besides, you didn't have a choice."

She looked up at him and smiled. "No, I didn't. Jonathan."

The car let them off in front of his building, and he held her close as the elevator whisked them to his floor. She got undressed and into bed first, already drifting off by the time he climbed in and spooned around her.

In their earliest days together, the inches between their bodies might as well have been miles. Now, he could feel her breathing slow and deepen because she was pressed against him. He marveled at her intensity. The club, him and their young relationship, still trying to navigate her way forward from a tragedy so cutting, so life-changing, he could not imagine.

Every so often, he glimpsed moments of sadness flit across her face. Of course she still thought about Harris. Of course she missed him. It must be worse when she was alone or not busy. Maybe that's one reason Octavia chose her to fill in at the club—she thought it might help.

Man, if you had asked him six months ago if he would be okay with his girlfriend working at a BDSM club, he wouldn't have thought twice about his answer: Hell no.

But in a way he had the club to thank for how their relationship was progressing. Their play, their arrangement, their sex, their lovemaking had reached another new level.

Tonight, among so many people, they had shared such a private experience, a cloak of intimacy and trust wrapped tight around just the two of them.

The public thing had never interested him before. It might be hot to watch in a movie or to fantasize about, but it wasn't anything he aspired to in real life. Yet somehow, when pressed to define and voice his boundaries with her playing—or rather, not playing—with other members at the club, one thought had led to another, and the idea had come to him.

And then, when he had seen her black pencil skirt hanging on his closet door that morning, his brain took it a step further. Have something *accessible* custom made. Although the hands-through pockets had been awkward to explain to the seamstress, who agreed to work fast, they were a real stroke of genius. If he did say so himself.

Lightly, he kissed the back of her naked shoulder,

lingering long enough for her scent to reach his nostrils. She surprised him with a sleepy mewl and turned to kiss him. He stroked her cheek, a paper-light touch, and her mouth opened to him.

It may have been the most sexy kiss of his whole life.

He wrapped his arms around her, cupped the back of her neck, pulled her on top of him as she kissed down his neck and nuzzled her face in the crook of his shoulder. Her breathing was still slow and deep.

Her hips pressed toward his, her hand searching for him. Holding her cheeks, he guided her. His dick felt her moisture. If he had realized she was this wet, he might not have let her fall asleep so fast.

She took hold of him, raised and angled her hips, and . . . 99 . . . 98 . . . 97 . . . enveloped him.

He held onto her ass but let her lead. The rawness of her movements cast a spell he didn't want to break. And soon she was whimpering and tightening around him, which set off his own climactic pulsing inside her.

He withdrew and guided her beside him again. Her breathing slowed into sleep as she curled up against him, their legs tangled under the sheets.

This woman.

He dozed and woke a few times, restless, and glanced at the clock. Two nineteen. He needed to sleep. He needed to be fresh early tomorrow to get his shit together for his meeting with Charles.

Charles made Becca happy, which was reason enough for Jonathan to like him. But he truly seemed like a good guy. After all, he was getting married Saturday, but as soon as Jonathan reached out, he had agreed to a short meeting.

Jonathan wanted to pick his brain. With the amount of globetrotting Charles did and all his connections, he no doubt would have ideas, suggestions, avenues to pursue. And with the reputation of his family's firm, should Demeleo Investment Group decide to back Jonathan's idea, the affiliation would give him a leg up with other investors too.

He hadn't told Quinn any more about starting his own production company, and he hadn't told her about his meeting with Charles. Better to wait to see how things evolved and, if they hewed to plan, surprise her with great news.

A WEDDING

Twenty-eight round tables dotted the wood floor of the sunlit barn, each set with ivory cloths and gold chargers. The centerpieces overflowed with colorful blossoms in fall shades—salmon and rosewood and burgundy. Soft green eucalyptus and sultry wild raspberry accented each mammoth arrangement. The florist left only an hour ago, and already the fragrance of fresh-cut flowers filled the space.

Ten chairs sat perfectly spaced around each table, bows and tails of ivory organza trailing down the backs, a formal touch Becca thought would please Charles's parents. Three bartenders were setting up a long bar at the far wall. With chalk, Quinn had marked off the floor to guide them so they wouldn't encroach on the band or the buffet or the smooth parquet tiles laid for dancing.

She took another sweeping look around and exhaled a deep breath in relief. Everything so far had gone according to plan, and the barn sparkled with even more elegance and romance than she had imagined.

Just a few last items to cross off her list and then, her

hair and makeup done earlier this afternoon, she could run inside fast to change. She took the phone from the back pocket of her jeans and cupped her hand to block the sun's angled glare as she checked the time.

It was almost five o'clock. The ceremony would soon be underway in the city. Quinn had insisted on staying back to make sure everything was just how Becca wanted it. Leigh promised to send photos from the officiant's chambers.

From the barn's storage room, she retrieved the velvet-lined box with Becca and Charles's engraved cake knife and an extra extension cord for the caterer, then set out the blackboard easel welcome signs along the driveway. In Jerome's car, polished lovingly to a sheen and parked outside the stone gate, she tucked the key under the driver's floor mat for Charles.

Check, check, check, and check.

As she headed toward the house to change, she looked up at the sky.

Thank you.

Mother Nature had smiled. When Quinn woke up this morning, thick, cold, gray fog hung in the valley, and the forecast called for showers. Indeed, it had sprinkled a few times, enough to make her store the blackboard signs inside and leave the convertible top up. But by lunchtime the remaining clouds had skittered away, revealing a crisp blue autumn sky.

Becca was lucky in many ways, and Quinn was glad for that. Growing up without her father around, and with Leigh such an exacting single parent, couldn't have been easy. Neither woman talked about Becca's dad. In all the years Quinn had known them, not once had they mentioned that part of their past. One time at some publishing event, someone asked Leigh if she had ever been married. She simply said no and abruptly changed the subject.

Whatever had happened, Quinn assumed that story was at least in part behind Leigh's drive and focus, behind her lack of emotionality and at times frustrating lack of empathy. But Quinn had never asked. Friends gave friends space. If or when Leigh, or Becca, wanted to share, they would.

In many other respects, mother and daughter differed like night and day. Where Leigh was reserved, Becca radiated warmth. Where Leigh's expressions rarely betrayed her true feelings, Becca wore hers on her sleeve. When Leigh asked Becca a long list of questions about Charles when they met during a study-abroad semester in London, Becca had—as Leigh told it—rolled her eyes and said none of that mattered, that the two of them just fit.

Quinn's phone chimed, and she turned it over to see a text and photo from Leigh.

Can you believe it !?!

The picture showed Becca and Charles from behind as they stood on the marble staircase of City Hall, about to go up. In a dapper gray suit, he rested his hand at the base of Becca's back, exposed by the diamond cutout of her exquisite ivory dress. The wedding party gathered around them—handsome groomsmen and gorgeous bridesmaids, smiles brimming with delight.

Quinn's thumbs moved fast.

Beautiful.

She added a happy-tears emoji.

A few moments later, Leigh sent another photo. Becca and Charles facing the officiant, once again their backs to the camera. Leigh had captured their interwoven hands, their heads leaned close, each resting against the other.

A wave of heaviness crested in Quinn's chest as she pictured her and Harris's wedding almost twenty years ago, also at City Hall on a crisp, clear day.

A wedding today would have made him happy, all the happier if he were officiating. At the thought of him, she circled back to the side of the barn, to the peony bushes she'd brought from the old house and planted.

She had taken a break from the preparations this morning and sat here beside them, the edges of their green summer leaves turning red as the season changed, another example of the unyielding march of time.

She kissed the tip of her index finger and touched it to a leaf. "I miss you," she whispered. But she would not succumb to sadness today. Today was about Becca and Charles and joy.

Her phone chimed and buzzed with more photos from Leigh and from Jonathan too—Becca and Charles leaving City Hall, kissing amid a cloud of glittering gold confetti, their clasped hands in the air showing off their wedding bands.

In the house, she changed into her dress, a simple burgundy sheath with a low cowl in front and back. The gentle folds at the neck had caught her eye from the window of a boutique near Octavia's.

Leaning closer to the bedroom mirror, she swiped lipstick and pressed her lips together to smooth the color, then slipped the tube into her black wristlet. The patio heaters she rented would warm the barn, but she slid the black cashmere wrap off its hanger to bring with her for when the temperature dipped outside later tonight.

Soon, she heard car doors slamming, the stop and start of engines as the first guests arrived and valets whisked the vehicles away to be parked. By the barn's large double sliding doors, she greeted the visitors—no one she knew yet —before following them inside.

One of the women stopped with a sharp intake of breath, and the others halted beside her, their eyes growing wide. Quinn had helped the contractors decorate all day, but now she tried to see the space through the guests' eyes. It really was magical—billowing fabrics draped over the beams; tall, full bunches of flowers; strings of twinkle lights and hanging lanterns; hammered copper champagne buckets refracting the light.

She chatted with the waves of arriving guests as the barn filled with scents, with movement, and with sound— singular voices, excited conversations, wine corks popping, beverage cans' metallic cracks and hisses. Plates and silverware clanked as wait staff began to circulate with trays of hors d'oeuvres.

A hand tugged her shoulder, and she turned. Leigh was standing beside her, eyes glassy and red.

"I can't tell you how fabulous this is. I mean . . . we talked about it, but I didn't envision . . . this." Leigh gestured around the barn, now bustling.

"It is fabulous—and we pulled it off together," Quinn said, feeling a sudden swell of affection. Despite her issues with Leigh, they had a history too long and close to cast aside. Their relationship might be changing, but today would be one of the most memorable days of Leigh's life, watching her daughter marry a man she loved wildly.

And Quinn was sharing it with them. Today, nothing else mattered but that.

Leigh shook her head in wonder as she scanned the barn again, then pulled Quinn into a spontaneous hug. "Becca's going to lose it when she sees what you did."

———

QUINN AND JONATHAN stood near the barn doors chatting with a guest when they heard it, the engine of Jerome's car turning over, sweet and smooth as honey. That's just how he had reported it to her this morning, after he motored down the driveway and parked it by the street.

Excitement fluttered through her as guests streamed out of the barn and lined up on both sides of the drive, clapping and cheering while the old Bel Air puttered through the stone pillars. The tin cans she'd been scavenging for weeks clattered over the bumps and the rocks.

Charles had the wheel; Becca perched on the seat back beside him, one hand on his shoulder, the other holding her bouquet. He drove slow and controlled, the best kind of tension rising.

They stopped just outside the wide barn doorway, smack dab amid the crowd. He cut the engine, and they waved at the people who treasured them.

He hopped out while Becca stood on the seat, placing one high-heeled foot on the doorframe. Someone wolf-whis-tled and laughter burst into the air like fireworks. Charles came around the car to meet her and, in one impressive swoop, cradled her in his arms.

Guests moved aside to give them access to the barn doors, and he stepped theatrically over the threshold. Their lips locked as first one shiny black loafer, then a second, touched down on the other side. The two of them beamed as he set her to her feet, and loving chaos ensued as the raucous crowd swarmed to congratulate them.

They made an arresting couple. Becca looked beatific in her dress, with its high neck of tiny ivory pearls accentuating her face, which was aglow and framed by ringlets. Her bare arms were toned and strong. She was nearly as tall as Charles, who was just as handsome in person as Quinn had seen from the sporadic photos Leigh had shared in the past.

After hearing so much about him from Becca and Leigh, she felt like she knew him, especially watching him now, joshing it up with his friends.

The incredible lightness of relief at seeing the pleasure on so many faces buoyed her. All the planning and organizing, the extra phone calls to double- and triple-confirm details to make sure nothing would go wrong—it was so worth it. Now here they were, Becca and Charles married, their shared life brimming wide with possibility.

A GROOMSMAN BROKE AWAY from the crowd to retrieve a bottle of champagne from a nearby standing bucket. He popped the cork and everyone cheered as the bubbly liquid frothed.

With one arm around Becca's waist, Charles took the bottle by the neck from his friend's outstretched hand and brought it to her lips to take a sip, then took a swig himself and wiped the overflow with the back of his hand. Quinn leaned close to Jonathan, felt his unrestrained laugh. All around them, joy—like the fizzy champagne previously trapped in a bottle—overflowed.

After more drinks and appetizers, everyone found their

seats and raised their glasses in the official toast by Charles's best man.

A talented harpist friend of Becca's performed during dinner. Quinn and Jonathan sat with Leigh's friends, along with Charles's sister, brother-in-law, and their two adorable kids. It was a chatty, friendly group, and one of the rare times Quinn wasn't hating the small talk.

While the guests ate, Becca and Charles circulated, stopping at each table to visit. When they got to Quinn and Jonathan's, Charles's niece bounced up from her seat like only a six-year-old could. "Uncle Chuck!" She reached for him, and he scooped her up.

"Riley! How's my favorite niece?"

"Good! I'm your *only* niece, silly."

"Oh, that's right," he deadpanned. "But you're still my favorite."

"And you're my favorite uncle." She giggled, proud of her quick comeback. "When the good music starts, can we dance? You too, Aunt Becca!"

Clearly, she hadn't developed an ear for classical music. "This *is* good music—don't you like it?" he asked.

She shrugged sheepishly, as if realizing she might offend the grown-ups. "It's too slooooow for dancing."

"I see." His dry humor was funny, how he kept a straight face with her. "Yes, when the hip music comes on, meet Aunt Becca and me on the dance floor. We should start practicing for *your* wedding." He leaned in conspiratorially. "Is there anyone special?"

She didn't hesitate, turning to whisper into his ear— loud enough that the whole table could hear—"Connor. He's also in first grade. But you have to promise not to tell."

Charles raised an eyebrow at her parents as if to ask if they knew about Connor.

"Don't worry," he told her, pretending to turn an imaginary key at his lips. "I'm a master at keeping secrets."

Leigh had often spoken of wanting grandkids, and Becca had alluded to children as the three of them planned the wedding. It was obvious he and Becca would make loving parents.

The meal ended, and the servers carried trays piled with empty plates back to the catering trailer. While the DJ set up by the dance floor, the harpist played her last piece. More string lights that Quinn had set with timers flicked on, bathing the barn in a dreamy, golden glow.

Soon the DJ's deep voice boomed. "Let's give it up again for the briiiiide and groooom, Rebeccaaa and Chaaarles." Riley vibrated with excitement as the two of them made their way hand-in-hand through the standing crowd, their first dance as husband and wife.

AS THE LAST notes of Becca and Charles's song led into the first notes of the next, Jonathan joined Becca on the dance floor while Charles walked to the edge where his mother stood. He extended his forearm to escort her out to join them.

It was so sweet of Becca to have asked Jonathan to dance with her. The music was slow and sentimental but loud, and he leaned close so she would hear him. "So, Mrs. Demeleo, how has your day been?"

She leaned back to look at him before answering. "My day has been a-*mazing*." Moisture glistened along her lower eyelids, and she waved her hand by her face. "Sorry, it's just . . ." She gestured around the barn. "Look at this. Every time I think about what Quinn did for us, I get choked up."

"It is incredible. And you. I've never seen a more beautiful bride. How did you grow up so fast—and so well?"

She laughed at that. "I had a wonderful village around me. Remember how you took me to the network's take-a-kid-to-work days, and when you were shooting in New Orleans? And *Rome*? What kid gets to do that kind of stuff? Thank you." She leaned against him, and they danced in comfortable silence.

Once he was back at the table and sitting beside Quinn again, he watched Becca and Charles out there dancing with their friends. It was hard not to grin. They seemed crazy about each other.

A knot of guilt and regret tightened in his gut. He should have been crazy in love at his wedding. But regret without change was for pussies; he was a different man now than he was back then.

He put his hand on Quinn's thigh, half resting on her silky dress, half on her bare leg where the fabric stopped. Assuming she agreed, he hoped one day in the not-too-distant future he might get to experience being madly in love at his wedding.

At the next slow song, he took hold of her hand. "May I have this dance?"

"Of course. Jonathan." She smiled demurely as they headed to the dance floor. She didn't hold on to him the formal way, but kept her hands around his neck as they swayed to the music.

The surrounding sounds faded, and his skin tingled under her touch. "Except for the bride, for obvious reasons, you are the most magnificent woman in this room," he whispered in her ear. "You look ravishing."

He wanted to dance her to the darkest corner of the barn and slide his hands under her hemline. She looked up at him with a teasing smile, one eyebrow cocked—she probably felt him getting hard. "Don't even *think* about it. You promised. Jonathan."

"You asked, but I don't believe I actually agreed." He tip-toed his fingers around her waist, tugged gently on her dress as if he were going to lift it.

"Don't you dare. I'm serious." Her eyes pleaded, although she also was trying not to smile.

"I forgot to tell you not to wear panties. Are you?"

"Yes. Jonathan. I'm wearing panties." She lowered her voice when she said *panties* and took hold of his lapels, flattened her hands against his chest while they continued to move to the music, one of her legs between his, one of his between hers. He would like other parts of his body between her legs, but he would not stress her out tonight.

"Then I think you should be punished."

That same expression—a mix of playfulness, desire, and a hint of fear—spread across her face once more. "Okay. Jonathan. Just not now. Not here. Later tonight, okay?" She cupped his cheek, ran her fingers along his jaw.

"Tonight? You'll be exhausted later." He stroked the side of her head. He loved how her hair felt against his hand. And how it smelled—he was going to look into buying a lifetime supply of that product.

"Okay, then another time. Whenever you want."

"You know what I want?" The idea just hit him, and it was a great one.

Her hands moved back around his shoulders, her gaze returning to his. "Tell me, Jonathan."

"I want a whole day with you," he said without hesitation, without asking. "Consider it your *Day* of Punishment."

It would be like a date-night but an entire day. He could set up a mini dungeon in his guest room.

He watched her process what he said. Slowly, she nodded and gave him a nervous look that turned flirty and daring and hungry.

"How about a week from this Monday? Octavia will be back by then and, besides, the club's closed on Mondays."

THE CROWD HAD THINNED CONSIDERABLY, the remaining guests relaxing further with each song, each dance, each bottle of wine and fit of laughter. Suit jackets hung over chair backs, the seats no longer neatly arranged.

At Quinn's table, and most of the others, napkins lay scrunched in a heap after their owners got up to socialize and refresh drinks and dance. Pairs of high heels sat beside chair legs, abandoned for flip-flops or bare feet.

It was disorganized, messy, and buoyant.

Jonathan stood by the bar talking to an acquaintance. Becca sat on a wayward chair by the edge of the dance floor, chatting with a friend. Neither Charles nor the groomsmen were around; they must already have gone outside.

She ducked into the house to grab the s'mores supplies in the big tote bag on the kitchen counter. Outside, the torches along the path threw off enough light for guests to get safely to the bathrooms and to the deck by the river. But a light string draping the deck rail flickered, so she detoured to check the connection.

From the deck, she could make out Charles and his friends by the stone ring, nurturing the campfire. Cell-phone flashlights shined sword-like rays. It was dark down there. The extra garden torches she ordered were stored behind the barn, where she headed to fill their reservoirs with fuel. On her way to the fire pit, she grabbed a gas lighter from the shelf with her free hand and headed toward the group to help.

She worked each torch into the ground on her way to the guys. As she lit the wicks, they looked in unison in her direction. "Let there be light," she called. "Now you can see what you're doing."

They already had put their jackets over every other wood stump, chivalrously covering the seats for the ladies.

Sweet.

Charles rose from kneeling by the hissing, crackling logs and waved.

"Quinn. I have to tell you—you've made my wife and me astoundingly happy today. Thank you. Although that sounds inadequate."

A chord of familiarity resounded in her mind. His voice? She couldn't put her finger on it. "I was delighted to do it. Becca feels almost like a daughter to me and, to be honest . . ." *It's his wedding day. Don't talk about Harris.* "It's been good to have a positive focus. I should thank the two of you."

Abruptly, as if he felt uncomfortable or just remembered something—or maybe he was shy—he lowered his gaze and knelt again by the fire. One of his friends came over and handed him a beer. As he reached up to take it, the shirt sleeve that had been folded back near his elbow shifted. She looked once, twice. If she had been standing just a half-step away, she wouldn't have seen it. The angle would have been wrong; it would have been obscured by a shadow or the darkness.

Unfortunately, she wasn't a half-step away, and she did see it: Just inside the crook of his elbow was the same uneven patch of scarring she had noticed at the club, on Maximillian's arm.

IT'S DARK. *He can't be the only one in Manhattan with a scar. Even with the same contours. Even in the same spot.*

Charles looked at her, and his expression stole her disbelief. He swallowed. "Worlds collide," he said under his breath.

"That, they do."

He stood again, ready to say something.

"Oh, there you are!" Becca trooped down the path, her voice bubbly and smiling. "I've been looking all over for you." He put the arm Quinn had been eyeing around Becca's waist and brought her in for a kiss.

"Hey, Beautiful. Did you miss me?"

"Of course I did," Becca cooed. "You're my *husband*."

"And you're my *wife*," he cooed back, kissing her again.

Quinn imagined him saying the words with a British accent and a wave of nausea rose in her stomach. Becca giggled. "Let's not make people sick," she said, pulling slightly away. "Especially this lady."

Becca turned to Quinn. "I've been trying to get you two in the same place all night. I see you've finally met Charles." Then she faced him. "Honey, as you know by now, this is Quinn, who not only saved our bacon but organized The. Most. Incredible. Wedding."

She turned back toward Quinn. "It's so much nicer than our original plan—it makes me believe some things do happen for a reason. I *ne-ver*—" she lowered and slowed her voice as she repeated the word—"thought I would say that after our building flooded. Frankly, I don't know how we'll ever be able to thank you enough."

She hugged Quinn and kissed her cheek while Charles

met her gaze over Becca's shoulder. "Becca is right. It's incredible."

Quinn hoped Becca didn't feel her tension. No one other than Jonathan—and now Charles—knew about her belonging to Octavia's, and she wanted to keep it that way. She was not embarrassed or ashamed, but she knew others, like Leigh for instance, would—did—not understand.

She took a steadying breath and forced a smile. "The best thank you of all would be for you two to have a long, happy life together."

A woman's voice Quinn didn't recognize yelled for Becca from up near the barn. "We plan to," Becca said, pecking Charles's cheek, then Quinn's. With that, she gathered the fabric of her dress at the thigh and ran off.

Becca.

Quinn had not seen Becca at the club with Charles. She pictured the woman with the collar, the one in the harness of knots he played with, but she had not seen Becca at Octavia's.

Calm down.

Charles remained standing beside Quinn, the crackling fire behind them. His voice was low when he spoke. "Kayla. I see the questions written all over your face. But now isn't the time."

He was watching something behind her. "Ah, my lovely mother-in-law," he said as Leigh joined them. "You just missed Becca. We were telling Quinn how grateful we are for what she's done."

Leigh put a fawning hand on Charles's upper arm and leaned against him. "Can you believe how great he is?" she said to Quinn.

He threw his arm around Leigh's shoulder and gave her

a sideways hug. Another wave of nausea rose in Quinn's gut.

"I really *can't* believe it. He should have a twin."

———

BECCA, Leigh, and Charles tottered into the barn, smiling and disheveled—it was close to two a.m. "We were just coming to find you two," Becca said, her voice hoarse. "We're heading out, but I have a surprise."

Please, not another one.

She and Jonathan walked the three of them to the car that would take them to Leigh's apartment to rest for a few hours before their flight to Tahiti. Those hours were rapidly dwindling, but adrenaline no doubt would keep them awake tomorrow no matter how little they slept.

Becca and Leigh couldn't stop thanking her. Charles smiled and vocalized his agreement, but otherwise stayed quiet.

"Could you pop the trunk, please?" Becca asked the driver before turning to Quinn. "Close your eyes."

She heard Becca rustling, and the trunk lid slammed shut. "Okay, you can open your eyes."

When she did, Becca stood before her, holding her bouquet. "This is for you. I didn't throw it—I wanted to make sure it went to you."

Becca's eyes welled as she handed over the gorgeous flowers. "What you did for us was so amazing, especially after what happened. It couldn't have been easy thinking about a wedding, about every single minute detail of a wedding. I know it's just superstition"—she gestured to the blossoms, still fragrant, the stems and petals still firm and fresh—"but I hope they bring you another true love."

"Oh, sweetie, come here." Quinn hugged her tight. "Thank you." She fought back tears at Becca's poignant gesture.

When they moved apart, Charles put his arm around his wife's shoulders. He gently kissed the top of her head, resting his cheek there momentarily, breathing her in as if he, too, were moved by her thoughtfulness.

Quinn tried to read his emotions. Fear, nervousness, guilt, sheepishness, smugness, indignation, regret—any feeling she would expect if he were hiding something from Becca. But she detected not an inkling, just adoration, gratitude, love.

She had let her mind wander far and wide these past few weeks, trying to foresee and prevent every potential wedding glitch and what-if—heavy rain, muddy grounds, a blackout, or no-show DJ. Wasp stings, allergies, food poisoning, a fall. She never would have guessed this.

It had been the picture-perfect wedding for a couple clearly, deeply in love.

Exactly.

Her shoulders relaxed. There had to be an explanation for why Charles had gone to the club alone. Maybe he and Becca had an agreement, or an open relationship. Maybe she belonged to a different club. Maybe she didn't go to any club. Maybe she was more like Jonathan—or Preet's wife—preferring to keep their play at home, but she was fine with Charles going. The details didn't matter. What the two of them did privately, and the pacts couples made inside a marriage, were none of Quinn's business.

But suddenly, looking at them together, she was certain and relieved about this one thing: Becca knew.

QUINN AND JONATHAN watched from the kitchen window as the catering truck headed down the driveway, its blinker flashing in the darkness. "So, Ms. Wedding Planner, are you satisfied with how tonight turned out?"

"It was great. People raved about the food and the gorgeous cake, the music, the decorations, the car—everyone loved that old car—and Becca . . ." Quinn's eyes grew watery again. "She looked so beautiful, so happy, didn't she?"

"She did. There is something very special between them; you can feel it." He squeezed her hand.

It had been horrible of Quinn to even for a single second entertain the crazy idea that Charles might have some secret life.

In her defense, she had been a ball of nerves trying to make today perfect and she was exhausted, but still. Of course Becca knew. Of course she and Charles would share something that big, that important.

If anyone could be accused of hiding something, it was Quinn.

She hadn't leveled with Leigh or Becca while they were planning the reception—for goodness' sake, she snuck off to Paris and hadn't said a peep to either of them. Maybe she was projecting her own worries about others' reactions onto poor Charles.

She reminded herself she had also been mistaken about Jonathan and Delphine. She squeezed his hand back. Becca and Charles just had a wonderful send-off for their life together. And now, what mattered most was this man standing beside her, holding her hand, this man who made her heart race.

The red light on the house phone blinked, and he

leaned against the counter next to her while she entered the voicemail code.

"Hey, kids." It was Becca, giggling, sounding a little drunk. "Surprise! By now, you two better be doing something dirty. Buuuut, in case you need a push, here you go—"

The sound of metal clinking glass—Quinn pictured her tapping a spoon to a champagne flute—came through the cordless handset. With the background road noise, the three of them still must have been in the car back to the city.

"Did you get that?" Becca yelled. The glass tinked several more times, rustling ensued, and then the line went quiet. She imagined Charles taking the glass out of her hands, putting his arm around her, shaking his head while he laughed and ended the call.

Jonathan laughed too, the sparkle in his eyes sharpening. She put the phone in its cradle, stepped between his legs, and put her hands on that familiar warm, broad chest. Becca's words when she handed her the bouquet earlier replayed in her head. *I hope they bring you another true love.* "As the wedding planner, I believe it's my duty to make sure we do not disappoint the bride."

"We should definitely not disappoint the bride." His voice was husky and tired and happy as he held her face tenderly and leaned down to meet her lips.

BTW, NO PANTIES

Quinn sat at Octavia's desk finishing a sandwich while scrolling the calendar. Relief. Only two more days at the club. The ring of her mobile drew her gaze away from the computer monitor, to Octavia's name scrolling across the phone screen.

She sounded like she was in a wind tunnel, and Quinn felt her face squinch in concentration. "It's hard to hear you —you're breaking up."

" . . . Pretty intense . . . one more week . . . experimental treatment . . . Please . . . sorry . . . Thank . . ."

The call dropped. Quinn tried to call her back, but it went straight to voicemail. Great.

The sound of a whip cracking redirected her attention— Octavia's programmed alert for new arrivals. She checked the monitor showing the vestibule camera feed. It was a wired system rather than wireless, Octavia had explained during a club tour, a deliberate choice to minimize the risk of hacking, which could reveal member identities.

But this particular arriving member Quinn knew, inside

the club and, since the wedding, outside. His stature and firm jaw, the camel wool coat, the expertly tailored suit underneath—she watched in black and white as he swiped his membership card to unlock the inner door to the private changing room. When he emerged from the other side onto the club's main floor, no doubt he would be wearing his mask.

A few moments later, the whip sound cracked again. This time a woman entered the vestibule, the collared woman she had seen before with Charles, the nearly naked collared woman, up on level three. Quinn stopped herself from reading the name scrolling along the bottom of the monitor—better not to know.

What she did know was that there was always more to the story of any relationship than others knew.

Her phone vibrated against the desk. Octavia reaching out again, she hoped.

Instead, it was a text from Jonathan.

> In the neighborhood. Just finished lunch with a potential investor. It's looking good. Can you take a coffee break? Meet at that cafe down the street from the club?

> That's fantastic news! I'd love to, but there are members here. Tonight, your place?

> Mid-day? Bondage never sleeps. Or works, I guess.

> No. ;)

> Good to know. Will remember.

> I bet you will. Jonathan.

Can I take you to dinner later?

If I can get a DM to cover, yes.

Make it happen. Vieve? 7:30?

I will try. Sounds lovely.

Vieve was a cozy French bistro with excellent food in a less-traveled corner of the city. Octavia had mentioned it, said it reminded her of Paris, that she and Quinn should have dinner there sometime.

That warm, fluttery feeling Jonathan never failed to evoke unfurled in her chest. Warm, fluttery feelings unfurled lower, too, as she thought back to Leigh's author event and their encounter on the terrace.

She caught herself smiling. Whatever he had in store for dinner, she would like, including simply sitting across from him over candlelight and catching up on their days. She would tell him about Octavia's call and that she had to fill in for another week.

He was understanding and patient; he might not love the idea, but they were making it work in their own way.

She also wanted to tell him about Charles, but she could not do that until she talked with him first about this surprise crossing of paths.

Then, once she did, it would be out in the open. Not that she wanted to discuss her involvement at the club or share details of her and Jonathan's sex life with Becca and Charles. But at least it wouldn't be a big secret that three of them knew and Jonathan did not.

She worked on the main floor, checking the items off Octavia's pre-event checklist to help the DMs working the bondage seminar tonight. She slowed each time she passed the staircase, hoping to bump into Charles on his way down. All she needed was a minute for them to talk.

No such luck.

Later, back in Octavia's office, she glanced at the monitor and caught Charles going from the dressing room to the exit vestibule to leave. She wished there was a speaker she could use to tell him to wait. His Maximillian mask was off now, and he tapped away on his phone screen as he walked, smiling. Good news about a deal? A joke from a friend? Telling Becca he was leaving the club and on his way home?

Her phone droned against the desk again, and she grabbed it. Maybe this time it was Octavia.

Nope, not Octavia, but Jonathan again.

BTW, no panties.

HE WANTED to stop by the club even though she was busy. He would only stay a minute, give her a kiss, and leave. But especially now, on the cusp of this new opportunity, of rebuilding his career, he couldn't risk it.

The follow-up meeting with Charles earlier today had gone well, and Jonathan was going to submit the more detailed version of his business plan that would, he hoped, lead to a deal memo. If something blew up on social media, like visiting a BDSM club, for example, it wouldn't look great. And he didn't want to give Charles any reason not to back this venture.

Instead, he would see Quinn in a few hours, sit across from her at the secluded table he reserved in one of Vieve's private alcoves, with curtains and a chandelier that cast soft, sexy light. She would love it.

And with the extra privacy the curtains afforded, well, he would take full advantage of the situation and make sure she enjoyed that, too.

As soon as he got back to the apartment, he opened his laptop, typed some quick notes for himself about today's meeting, and opened the file with his list of potential advertisers and investors to add to the business plan.

Charles had encouraged him to be creative in building the list, and he had been. Not your typical bloated-network corporate sponsors but newer, more progressive companies, disruptors and innovators. He added a few more market segments that had occurred to him on the walk home, proofread it twice, three times, then drafted a cover email to Charles.

He reviewed the documents once more. Charles's support meant a lot. It could open more doors, get him the total investment he needed to produce pilot episodes for multiple series, which would give Jaines Productions a strong start out of the gate.

Don't overthink. Send the bloody thing already.

He hit "send" and sat back. Nothing to do now but wait. It might be days, weeks even. He would need to chill.

It was a good excuse for his brain to turn to Quinn and dinner. He would play with her in the restaurant and give her the punishment she was due when they got home. He couldn't remember now why she was supposed to be punished, but they had joked about it and he would follow through, seize every opportunity. A cane in the window of an adult fetish and toy shop had caught his eye as he walked past it earlier, although he didn't go inside— for the same reason he hadn't gone to Octavia's to see

Quinn. Now, he pulled up the shop's website on his laptop.

Same-day delivery in Manhattan. Perfect.

He clicked the cane into the virtual cart along with several other intriguing implements, pausing to watch the recommended videos about safety and technique.

Maybe when Octavia got back from Paris, he would ask her for some formal training.

Okay, now his concentration was shifting downward to where his dick strained against his fly. Imagining the feel of Quinn tight and wet around him, he rubbed one out in record time.

After, with a new ability to focus, he continued his shopping spree.

When his phone chimed with an alert, he picked it up to find a text from Charles. He ignored the Open icon and quickly set the phone down without reading. If the deal didn't work out, okay. He would make other connections, look for other opportunities.

He got up and paced, rubbed the back of his head.

Charles's decision did matter to him. A lot. The stakes were high; this was his career. Quinn was making a new life for herself, and he needed to do the same. He wanted her to know he *could* do the same; she was a not-insignificant part of his motivation. And here he was, teasing her about Octavia's members coming to the club mid-day when he had just jacked off at his computer instead of working— working toward a goal he had had for a long time but not possessed the balls to pursue.

He turned over the phone screen, adjusted his reading glasses, took a deep, nut-growing breath, and tapped to read the text.

7

SAFE WORD OR SILENCE

After the quick huddle with tonight's DMs, she and Alex did their walk-through. Ample rope supplies for the seminar. Fire room stocked. Medical room sharps container empty. Tall jars on the counters topped off to the white line with disinfectant. Harnesses free of tangles. Lifts and pulleys running smooth and quiet.

"I think we're all set, but text me if you need backup later," she told Alex. Hopefully they wouldn't; she was looking forward to an evening alone with Jonathan, an evening giving herself *over to* Jonathan.

In Octavia's office, she changed back into the clothes she had worn here this morning, a black skirt and floral-patterned top, and checked the mirror. Her hair was flat from the long day, so she brushed and tied it back and added a dash of color to her lips.

A quick rummage to confirm her phone was in her bag, and she was out the door.

Waiting for the light to change at the corner, she remembered the panties. If she hurried, she could get to the restaurant a minute early and slip into the ladies' room to take them off.

Or leave them on and risk the consequences.

The pedestrian light turned green, and she and the sea of humanity around her moved as one mass across the inter-section. Her bag tight under her arm, she felt the phone vibrate against her ribs just as she stepped onto the curb. As soon as the crowd thinned around her, she checked it.

> Change in plans. Come to my place instead.

> . . .

> I left something for you in the elevator call box.

> . . .

> Make sure it's in place when you arrive.

> . . .

> I. Will. Check.

> . . .

> Panties can stay on.

A flush of heat bloomed inside her. Whenever she thought she was too tired or preoccupied or busy to be turned on by him, there it was, the wetness.

The phone buzzed yet again.

> By the way, we're having guests for dinner.

—

BARNES, Jonathan's doorman, tipped his cap as he sent her up in the elevator. She opened the call box and there it was, a toy from the collection Jonathan had displayed on the bathtub ledge the other night.

But tonight wasn't going to be a quiet evening for two. They would have an audience, an audience she would need to interact with. Maybe one of the potential investors he mentioned? With a toy very likely vibrating inside her. The launch party roof terrace sprung to mind.

No, Jonathan. But their so-called arrangement had been her idea, and clearly he was loving it.

Lifting her skirt and moving the panel of her thong to the side, she inserted the toy, short with no on/off buttons, and prayed he didn't have a camera in the elevator—at least not one that anyone else in the building could access.

As the elevator opened onto the penthouse landing, she was greeted by Becca's unmistakable bubbly laughter. Charles's deep voice followed.

Oh, just perfect.

Jonathan was laughing too. She paused for a second to listen. No other voices. So far, it sounded like it was just the three of them. At least there was that.

She walked slowly toward them, trying to ignore the silicone in her body.

They were standing by his kitchen island while he cooked. "Hey, there she is," Becca called, and rushed over to hug her.

Charles followed, less enthusiastically. Quinn wanted to whisper that they needed to talk, but she would wait until they were alone.

Jonathan was bent, peering into the oven while stirring

a small saucepan on the burner above it with one hand, so she went around the island to greet him. He stood and kissed her on the lips, then playfully tapped her nose with his. There was a new energy about him. It made her glad she hadn't ignored his order about the toy.

Becca stood beside the island with her elbow resting on the stone. "So, where are you coming from?" She looked at Quinn, waiting for her to answer.

"Oh, just . . . a bunch of things." She could feel Jonathan's eyes on her, probably curious what she would say. And maybe she should just say it, just tell the truth.

At a dungeon.

But no—she had to talk to Charles first to figure this out. "Errands mostly. You know." *Making sure the fire room is stocked with approved candles and flame retardant mats, that the bolts on the bondage furniture are tight. Just the usual to-do list.*

"Hey, food's almost ready," Jonathan jumped in. With mitts, he took a pan out of the oven and set it on the stovetop. "Becks, more sparkling water? Charles, another drink before we sit down? And Quinn—what will it be?"

"A gin and tonic sounds great, but"—she noticed Charles motion to Jonathan as if to say, *I've got it.*

Charles took Becca's water glass and his tumbler from the island and headed toward the bar cart in the living room. "Don't worry, I'll help myself," Quinn said to Jonathan.

While she and Charles went to get the drinks, Becca joined Jonathan by the stove.

Quinn made a gin and tonic as Charles picked up the bottle of whiskey. "We should talk," she started, but he interrupted her with a look.

"Still not the time," he said, softly enough for the sound

to dissipate before it reached Becca and Jonathan clattering about in the kitchen. "But I trust we'll *both* keep each other's confidences until we have a moment alone to chat."

The immediate, nauseated feeling she had gotten at the wedding upon learning Charles's identity returned. What he just said? It did not bode so well.

But he must have his reasons—reasons Quinn obviously wasn't privy to. Yet.

Because she refused to believe Becca wouldn't know about Charles and Octavia's.

He poured his drink—at least two fingers—and Becca's fizzy water, while Quinn glanced over at Jonathan, who was busy ferreting something out of the fridge.

They all met at the table. Honeymoon talk and romantic photos from their trip to Tahiti ensued. A picture shimmied in Quinn's imagination—Charles tying Becca up in their over-water bungalow like he had bound that woman at the club.

Think about something else.

After everyone finished their first plates, Becca joked about needing a rest before seconds and excused herself to the powder room by the entry. Charles offered to top off drinks and refill water glasses with the pitcher Jonathan had left on the counter.

When she and Jonathan were alone at the table, he reached over and stroked the back of her hand with the side of his bent index finger.

"Go into the bedroom and wait for me," he murmured. "Panties off."

"*Now?*" Despite her hesitance, a shudder ran through her, set off by the heat in his gaze.

"Safe word or silence."

HE FOLLOWED SHORTLY BEHIND HER, closing the bedroom door just as she sat on the edge of the bed. "Uh-uh. Not like that. On all fours. Skirt up. I want access."

His words drew another release of moisture. He stood by his dresser unpacking a box, but his body was blocking the contents.

"Coincidentally, I had a few items delivered this afternoon and one of them"—he held up the box and swiveled his wrist back and forth, waving it at her—"is this set of plugs."

"But I already have—"

"Shh. From back-door-averse to seasoned pro, ten sizes. For your ever-expanding pleasure."

"Are you reading the package or is that your own play on words?" she asked, an attempt at much-needed humor.

"Quiet. Unless I ask you a question. Head down. Shoulders down." He put his hand between her shoulder blades to show her what he meant. Now her bare behind was sticking straight up in the air. Lovely.

He put the box on the bed. "I've been wanting to experiment with anal, especially after you told me about Madame Manon and her 'I want you to remember why you're in Paris' stunt but I sensed you weren't crazy about the idea. Is that right?"

"That's right and also, it's a lack of experience. Jonathan."

"Fortunately, that can be remedied. I'll let you choose which one." He began to knead her cheeks, and she tried not to think about the other two people also in the apartment, not so very far away. "Except for number one—that's off limits. My pinky is bigger than that." He spread her cheeks. "See?"

She gasped at the cold lube, but his finger teasing her was warming. Slowly, he pressed in and removed it, each time the tiniest nudge further. He reached around with his other hand and circled her nub with a finger. For this, he used her own lubrication; there was no shortage.

"For someone not crazy about the idea, you seem aroused."

She didn't say anything; it wasn't a question. He had taken another page from Manon's handbook.

"And you're rocking back and forth in time with my finger moving in and out of your ass, did you realize that?"

"No, I didn't, Jonathan."

"Do you like it?"

Now that she was conscious of her rhythm, she glided her hips back to meet his next movement. "Yes."

He stopped circling and carefully removed his finger, then slid the box toward her head so she could see the assortment. She missed his hands instantly.

"Pick one." His voice deepened with his own arousal. By now, she knew how it sounded.

She took number two out of its molded tray and held it up to him.

The lube spluttered and he spread her cheeks again. He worked the plug in and out, pressing more firmly each time. "Try to relax," he whispered, prompting her to focus on her breathing. "There you go. Push out." He pressed harder this time, until it was seated inside her.

He lay on the bed next to her and began playing with her pussy again, first sliding a finger along her folds, then pressing and stroking her engorged clit—this, on top of the toy that was still inside her from the elevator, and the plug.

The man was torturing her silly. Her rocking continued, more insistent. Despite its size, the plug felt thick inside her, and she arched back toward it. So much sensation from this and the toy and how he touched her—she was so close.

"I had a feeling you might like this. Was I right so far?" His smile was devilish, his eyelids heavy with hunger.

"Yes, Jonathan. You were right." He slid his finger along her lips again, teasing. She gasped, and he stopped. "Don't you dare come. Understand?"

"Yes, Jonathan."

"Yes, what?"

"Yes, I understand." She exhaled hard into the comforter and dropped her head. She was dangerously close. "I'm not to come."

"I'll signal you with three short pulses; after that, you can come. Any questions?"

"Can we please wait until they leave? Please. Jonathan."

He slapped her ass and although she couldn't see his face, she could hear his smile. "You already know the answer to that."

He cleaned her up, helped her to her feet, put her panties back on, and lowered her skirt. "I'm going to clean up myself and then get back to our guests." He gestured with his thumb toward the door. "I expect you'll follow in a minute?"

"I just need to fix my hair and make sure I don't have lipstick on my face. But yes, Jonathan."

As she walked to the mirror, the toy vibrated—quietly, thank goodness.

"Sound check. Testing. It's completely silent," he said from the doorway, that smile of his back again.

Reconvened at the table, Becca, Charles, and Jonathan took second servings and ate every bite, while she moved a few forkfuls around her plate and drank cold water, hoping to cool the flush in both sets of cheeks.

They talked some more—a new exhibit at Becca's gallery, another she had just visited at the Met, a new partner at Charles's firm. Quinn managed to focus enough to ask how Leigh was doing.

"She's good," Becca said. "She had an important client dinner tonight, or she would have come."

Even distracted by the vibrator and plug, the reality stung. She used to be the client Leigh prioritized.

It must have shown on her face because Becca picked up again. "That came out wrong. It was already scheduled, and the guy is from out of town, so she couldn't . . ."

"It's okay. I knew what you meant," Quinn said. The conversation drifted to other topics, and she noticed Jonathan glance at his phone and tap. Sure enough, the vibe turned on, a slow, pulsing beat that drew her hips forward into the sensation no matter what her mind said.

As the conversation continued around her, he played.

He ramped it up, up, up—thank goodness even on the high settings it stayed quiet—then turned it off. When she nodded and made a short comment in response to something someone said—a short comment being all she could manage—he slow-danced it while she spoke.

Charles got up and offered to refresh drinks once more. Becca excused herself yet again to pee. While they were gone Jonathan sat back and, without moving his gaze from hers, tapped what must have been every single combination and permutation of pulse and vibration possible.

As Charles returned, she reached for her ice water and lifted it shakily to her mouth. Jonathan tapped again and put the phone face down on the table. Her sex was electrified; her ass squeezed around the plug.

It was delightful and horrifying at the same time. Charles put his glass on the table and sat across from her again, giving her a funny look, although she hoped beyond hope she was being paranoid.

Becca soon re-joined them, and the conversation continued. Jonathan's phone stayed put. She relaxed and took another sip of water, fingertips white from clutching the glass.

When he rose to clear the plates and bring dessert, she followed him, eager for a moment away from the guests. As she was loading the dishwasher, the wave began to swell. The toy pulsed slowly with a layer of vibration over the beat that grew faster and more rumbly every few seconds. The utensils fell into the dishwasher's basket and she straightened up, grabbing hold of the edge of the counter. Now, he was using a kitchen torch to caramelize the sugar on four ramekins of crème brûlée, the phone a few feet away on the island.

He raised an eyebrow at her. "Hands-free."

The intensity continued to rise. She crossed her legs and squeezed, hoping the island was blocking anyone else's view. He brought the dessert over to it and set it there, then tapped the phone. It stopped—the pulsing, the vibration— and she thought she might cry, whether from relief or frustration, it was hard to say.

And then she felt it, three vibrating thumps.

No, not here.

"Excuse me," she blurted, turning to run for the bathroom. He caught her wrist and mouthed, "Right here."

She tensed to stave off the wave about to crash. He opened the door of the refrigerator, a commercial model with tall, wide doors, thank goodness, and stood next to it to create a shield. Then he motioned for her to move closer so she could stand in the space he created.

Was he crazy? No, she shook her head. The toy might be silent, but Becca or Charles could easily wander over.

The symphony of heat and sensation began anew. Resistance was futile; she had no choice. Holding the edge of the countertop, she slid toward him just as that white hot force wrapped itself tight around her and she shattered.

"Give me a second," Jonathan called to his guests while she held onto the counter and tried to breathe quietly. The toy had stopped and the aftershocks were slowing, but she wasn't one-hundred percent sure her legs would function. Catching her eye, he closed the fridge door and stepped back, still—she really hoped—obscuring Becca and Charles's view. He nodded toward the hall.

She made a run for the bathroom and closed the door, then turned and leaned back against it, her body humming, swollen with so much stimulation.

After a few minutes, she went to the sink to splash cold water on her cheeks and clean up her makeup before teetering back down the hallway to rejoin his fiendish dinner party.

As she headed toward the three of them, he zapped the toy on and off, fast, multiple times, teasing her. Beads of sweat re-formed on her upper lip. She glared at him when she reached the kitchen and dining area. *Stop!*

He had worked her into such a state that, despite the orgasm five minutes ago, she might actually come again—or maybe the first was still in process. She had never experienced this before, so out of control of her own body. It didn't seem to matter that people were sitting at his dining room table.

He set the phone down on the island, although that

didn't assure her much peace; apparently, he could pre-program the app.

"Have a seat." He gestured to the table, pulled out her chair. Champagne now filled the flutes that had been added to each place setting in the short time she had been gone. Jonathan put his hand on her shoulder possessively.

"So, what's this big news?" Becca asked, looking at Quinn like she must know.

Good question.

"Wait, hold on a second." Fanning herself, she pushed her chair back. Just a short waddle to the terrace doors and she could breathe fresh air. "Hot flash," she lied. Jonathan smiled and stroked the back of her sweaty neck as she stood.

Once she was back at the table and seated again, he raised his glass and the three of them followed. "To friend-ship and success. Long-term, revenue-generating success."

"Here, here," Charles said.

Huh? The two men drained most of their glasses while Becca took a tiny sip. Quinn held onto hers with a less than steady hand. What exactly were they drinking to?

Charles nodded, indicating Jonathan should explain. He turned toward Quinn. "When I told you I met with a potential investor today, it was Charles. It looks like Demeleo Investment Group wants to invest in Jaines Productions. We'll be partners."

He leaned in and kissed her. "This means the company will have the money to pilot its first few series. Things moved quickly, and we talked again this afternoon. I didn't want to say anything to you until we shook on it, and now we have—I wanted to surprise you."

8

NO MORE FUZZY NEWBIE
HANDCUFFS

A couple of hours later, the elevator doors closed, Becca and Charles on their way home after what Jonathan had intended as a celebratory dinner. But Quinn's subdued reaction to his good news ate at him. Her eyes had bulged, she cleared her throat, she nodded, she forced an awkward smile. "Well, yes, that's . . . a surprise."

What the hell? Why wasn't she excited for him? Why wasn't she excited *with* him?

He knew this woman and, while he might not be able to read her exact thoughts, something about his announcement bothered her. That it would require him traveling again? She was busy; she had her own full schedule; she wasn't exactly sitting around pining to spend time with him. Or maybe it had nothing to do with the new series, and she was pissed about how he had made her come behind the fridge door? Or had something happened today at the club?

He walked toward the kitchen and paused as soon as she came into view, standing at the sink rinsing the rest of the dishes and putting them in the dishwasher. Even from a distance, he could see the tension in her neck, her shoulders. Her forehead, too, was tight. It looked like she was trying to work something out. But what?

He came up beside her and put his hand on her hip, angling her toward him. "Hey, let's leave it. I'll clean up tomorrow."

"I don't mind. You're going to be busy." Okay, so maybe it was about him not having as much time available. He let go of her hip and leaned against the counter beside her.

"What's on your mind? Are you upset about the toy, you know, with people around? Because, don't you trust me? I would never put you in a position to . . ."

"They were *right* there. I can't believe you did that." She expelled a short breath and shook her head. "But, yes, I trust you. Jonathan."

Good, so she wasn't so upset about that.

"There's something else then—you didn't seem excited about the news, about Demeleo." She was scrubbing a pot that was already clean. He took it from her, set it on the drying rack, and handed her a dishtowel to dry her hands. "Talk to me."

Her chest rose with a deep breath, and she nodded her head up and down several times fast. "I am. Excited for you. It's something you've wanted . . ." She trailed off.

"But?"

"That he's investing—that's huge. I'm surprised you didn't mention it. And we know them. Well. We have a lot of ties. We're like one big"—while her hands mimed a ball, her face twisted into a grimace. The word that sprang to his mind to capture what she was really thinking was *mess.*

"Web," she said, "like one big web. It's an important thing not to mention. And it's risky, taking money from someone you have personal ties to. His company is a big, fancy investment firm—is it going to be so different from working for a network? I know you can meet their expectations, it's just . . . I care about you. I don't want you to be unhappy."

Care about? He had been careful not to push the L-word discussion—neither telling her he loved her after that one time at the farmhouse, nor expecting or pressuring her to say it back. But hearing *care about* aloud, somehow it felt like a blow, a step backward, distant. Like she wasn't thinking of them as a unit, a couple; like to her, their lives were still separate.

Deciding to take the leap and go out on his own, to find an investor so he could create his own shows, it had a been a long-time dream of his, sure. But she had given him the confidence and the motivation to get off his rump and actually start *doing* it. It wasn't only for him; it was for the two of them. For a future, she just reminded him, he might be banking on more than she was.

"Exactly—we have ties. They're practically family. I thought that was a good thing. And we tentatively worked out some very fair terms. He said my business plan aligns well with where he wants to take the company when his father retires—this isn't some cut-throat, one-sided deal, Quinn."

He crossed his arms, realizing he probably looked like he was in a huff. Which he kind of was. "He's also been a big supporter of my work in the past, and the guy loves to travel. Lately he's been gone more than he's been here, right?"

She looked at him like she wanted to say something.

"What? Say it."

She hesitated. "I . . . I just wish you'd mentioned it sooner."

"I wanted to surprise you. Frankly, I've been feeling a little inadequate sitting home all day, unemployed, while you run Octavia's. I was excited to have good news to share with you. I thought you'd be happy for me. For *us*."

"I am happy." She was standing close but, mentally, she was miles away. Something was still bugging her. He stepped closer and reached for her, and she put her arms around his waist and leaned against him.

He held her tightly for a few moments, tension emanating from her. When she looked up at him, she had a different look in her eyes. *Need*.

It surprised him, given what he had done to her earlier this evening. Was it need for him? Need for escape? Need to forget? Were the answers as distinct as the questions, and did it matter anyway?

He held the side of her head, massaged her scalp with his fingers raking her hair. He tugged on the locks wrapped around his hand, releasing the scent of the goddamn raspberries that wiped his brain clear.

His doubts, his questions—they dimmed. She needed another release and she needed it from him. She might not be ready to think of herself as immersed in his future, but she was here, now, with him. He reminded himself again of how far they had come.

Whatever dark cloud had hovered over them a few minutes ago, it scudded away. He would give her more of what she craved—remind her that he could—and close the distance between them.

He kissed the top of her head. "This is good, Quinn, it's all good. I'm sorry I didn't tell you sooner, but it happened fast. It's not like I've been keeping something from you."

HE WALKED BEHIND HER, held her hands behind her back as they moved to the bedroom.

When they crossed the threshold, he eyed the pile of boxes on his dresser, the ones that had been delivered earlier. He had almost forgotten them sitting by the coat closet near the entry landing as he prepared for the impromptu dinner party. That would have made for some interesting conversation. *So what's in the boxes?* Becca would have asked.

Oh, nothing much, just a bunch of BDSM toys and equipment for Quinn—your typical same-day delivery items —anal plugs, a cane, stuff like that. No more newbie fuzzy handcuffs for us!

He could just picture the looks on their faces.

Many times he had wanted to go to the club—to bring Quinn a cup of coffee or lunch or, before she began her stint filling in for Octavia, to play with her, to be a part of her life there, to better understand. But each time, he stopped himself.

Although he hardly considered himself famous, people recognized him, especially in Manhattan, and he didn't want to risk it.

What would Charles think? *Wandering J. frequents BDSM club*—headlines and hashtags took on a trajectory of their own. It didn't matter how close to or far from the truth they landed. Being spotted also would bring attention to Quinn. Privacy was important to her, and to Leigh on Quinn's behalf, and he didn't want to jeopardize that.

In the bedroom, he clicked the thermostat up a couple degrees so she wouldn't get cold and walked her toward the bed.

"Clothes off," he whispered, dragging back the

comforter. "When you're done undressing, put your hands behind your back and keep your eyes closed."

She turned toward him and nodded. "Yes, Jonathan."

Hearing her voice alone got him hard, again. He had been trying to distract himself all evening, tried to ignore the discomfort of wanting her so badly.

Instead of leaving her so he could sort through the boxes for what he wanted, he watched her undress.

When she was nude and standing before him, he brushed his thumb under her eye like he had in the past to catch her tears. She wasn't crying, but that's where he was drawn, to the delicate skin there, to the weary eyes that held unspoken emotion. He kissed her, first softly at the corner of her mouth, then less softly full on. His hand around her neck, he let his mouth travel the territory of hers, kissing her full lower lip, tasting her upper one, letting himself get lost.

"Be right back," he finally told her and went to his dresser. He opened the longest box and found what he was looking for.

Then he went into the bathroom and took two thick towels from the shelf. One more stop at his closet for the overfull messenger bag—it was no longer large enough for their new level of play—and he took the blindfold, restraints, feather, and small leather flogger to the bed, placing everything but the blindfold on the floor beside it, where she couldn't see.

She was standing still, hands held behind her back, just as he had told her. He bent his head to suck on one gorgeous, attentive nipple before blindfolding her.

"Get on the bed, on your stomach," he ordered, guiding her so her head would be near the top of the bed. She moved gingerly.

The plug.

He was glad he had thought to use that earlier; thank you, Madame Manon. It was one more tool in his arsenal, one more thing to keep her from knowing what to expect or thinking he was too vanilla.

He bound one arm, then the other, one ankle, and the other to each of the bed's four legs, so she was spread-eagled. He stood still, looking at her—the waves of her hair, the rise of her shoulders and dip of her lower back, the curve of that fantastic ass, her long spread legs, and the treasure buried between.

But he would save his own sweet release a little longer.

From beside the bed, he took the feather and ran his hand from the quill to the tip, feeling its downy softness against his palm. He held it in one hand while in his other he took the birch cane—its long, thin strands held in place with a molded handle that fit his fist perfectly.

On his knees beside her, he gathered her hair and moved it over one shoulder so he could see her long neck.

That's where he started with the feather tip, at the spot just beside her shoulder. Her hand jerked, pulled back by the taut chain of the restraint. He stopped and massaged the ticklish skin until she relaxed, then started again. Her body tensed, but her arm stayed mostly still this time. "Good girl," he said.

Working his way down her body with the feather, he tickled and stroked and teased—her back, the sides of her breasts, the valley of her lower back and the top of her ass, the line between her cheeks—watching her small movements in response. The backs of her thighs, her knees, her calves, her ankles, her feet—her adorable, and probably tired, feet. When they tensed, he set the feather aside and took his time massaging them one by one, kneading the pads and spreading her toes with his thumb as if opening a fan.

He worked his way back up to her ass, tickling and massaging her calves and the backs of her thighs. Quietly, he put down the feather and picked up the cane.

When he swatted the fleshy, high curve of her butt cheek, she cried out. He could feel a welt rising even as he rubbed her skin to lessen the first sting.

"Are you ready for my instructions?"

She lifted her head to turn toward him. "Yes, Jonathan."

"When I tell you to start, I want you to count down from ten. You'll say one number at a time and not continue until you get a response from me. You won't say anything else but the numbers, or your safe word, or else I add five to wherever we are. Understand?"

"Yes, Jonathan."

"What's your safe word?"

"Red."

"Okay." He leaned over and kissed her temple, just above the fabric of the blindfold. "Start."

"Ten."

He swatted her other full globe with the cane, and she gasped. He sat on his hand so he wouldn't be tempted to rub the sting away this time. "Continue."

"Nine."

He did it again, the same cheek, intending to set her ass on fire, and sat back on his heels. A parallel red line formed. "Continue."

"Eight."

He did it a third time, same cheek but different spot, and sat back. "Okay."

"Seven."

He switched to the feather and tickled her foot with it. Her leg tensed, and he dragged the plume up the length of it, over her red cheek, and down the other leg, challenging himself to linger while still moving continuously toward her foot. When he lifted the feather off her skin and sat back on his haunches, he could see her leg muscles relax.

"Continue."

"Six."

With less force than he had applied to her behind, he caned the bottom of her foot. She let out a yelp. He did it again. "Conti . . ."

"Five." Was it his imagination, or was she in a hurry?

He hadn't planned to, but he flicked her foot with the cane again, then tickled his way up to her ass. A light brush down her center folds and more teasing over her back and along the length of her side. "Continue."

"Four."

"Take a deep breath and let it out slowly."

As she did, he gave her ass four slaps with the cane, three parallel lines and a cross-hatch. Her breathing sped up.

"Deep breaths." The air was still as he waited to hear several rounds of her longer inhale and exhale.

"Continue."

"Three." Her voice was starting to sound distant, dreamy.

He swatted the other cheek twice, then quickly followed with the feather. Her leg jerked the short distance of play allowed by the restraint. He rubbed her hot skin until she stilled, then he took a deep breath, let it out, and slapped her with his hand. Her gasp followed the smack of his palm; it had hit just right.

Beginner's luck.

Again he massaged, careful not to knead too hard. He had bought salve, but he was pretty sure she would still be sore tomorrow. As he moved around her ass, he let his fingers wander between her legs and glide slowly along the satiny wetness of her lips. He pressed the base of the plug, pushing it further, then released. Just to remind her it was there. To remind her he had put it there.

After undoing the restraints, he turned her over so she was on her back. One by one, he re-secured them, lightly running his nails over her limbs as he worked, making her shiver. "Continue."

"Two."

He took hold of her toes and caned the bottom of one foot, flicking his wrist lightly. Her toes curled and released and curled again when he swatted the other foot. Picking up the feather, he tickled her arch.

"No squirming."

Her head made a shushing sound against the sheet as she nodded. *Yes.*

"Do you want me to stop?"

Her *no* came out like a quiet wail. He traced the lines of her leg with the feather, around her ankles, up the long curves of her calf, around her knee, up and down and up her thigh, each stroke moving inward. He lifted the feather and moved to her navel, slowly teasing downward.

She writhed; he stopped, waited for her to still. When she did, he continued downward. With the lightest touch he could manage, he played the tip of the feather around her mound and folds. He stopped only to spread her further, to heighten her sense of exposure.

She moved toward him.

"Shhh. Stay still, or I stop."

She settled, but he could see her heartbeat racing against the skin of her neck.

"Breathe," he told her, sitting back, taking her in, watching that beating spot. Her pulse soon slowed, just like he wanted. He knew this woman, he knew her body, he knew how to rev her up and calm her down.

He waited a few more moments, the brief down time enough for his straining member to let him know it needed some serious up time.

Soon.

He wasn't done playing with her yet.

Silently, so she wouldn't know what he was going to do, he lifted the cane and smacked the bottom of her foot.

He had expected her to cry out; her moan surprised him. He swatted the same foot again. It must have hurt. This time, she expelled air where the moan had been. She was trying to be quiet.

"I'm changing the rules. I want to hear you."

"Yes, Jonathan." He swatted her foot again, trailed the cane up and down her legs, used it to tease her spread lips. She gasped. "Yes." Her hips tipped toward him, wanting. Asking.

"Do you want my fingers inside you?"

"Please. Jonathan."

When he complied, she cried out and he hardened even more against his fly at the sound, at the sensation of heat radiating from her center, at the sensation of the plug still. . .

"Jonathan. Can I come? . . . so close." Her words were clipped and breathless.

"No." He slid his fingers out quickly. "You haven't earned it yet." He spoke slowly, again picking up the cane and, lighter this time, swatted the bottoms of her feet to distract her.

Her uneven breathing and small movements slowed. While he waited for her to retreat from the edge, he undid the button of his jeans, the fly practically lowering itself from the pent-up pressure. A couple of strokes and he could come all over her, but he wanted to wait. He wanted to be inside her—inside her body, her heart, her life.

"What do you think? Are you ready for me to take you? To fuck you?" It came out softer and more tentative than he wanted. He still wasn't used to talking dirty to her. "With the plug still in you?"

"Yes, Jonathan. Yes."

He loosened all the restraints, positioned her on her hands and knees, and re-bound her wrists. Then he took off his pants, pulled her hips toward him, and slid into her velvety wetness, burying himself deep. The sexy sound she made almost had him coming on the spot.

. . . 99 . . . 98 . . . 97

"You feel . . . delicious." He thrust hard and fast, counting down as he did for distraction. He did not want this to be over anytime soon. A few years right here, her ass fitting perfectly into the bend of his pelvis, would be nice.

He leaned over and bit the soft skin beside her shoulder, nipped at the side of her neck, whispered in her ear. "Do you like it when I fuck you?"

That was exactly what he was doing—there was no polite way to say it. Hard, fast, deep. And she was taking him. All of him.

"Yes," she panted, "yes."

"Like this, with your hands bound, your body open to me?"

"Yes. Jonathan. I like it. Because I trust you." Her voice held pleasure and surrender at once, and it made his heart melt all over again.

Their rhythm escalated to a frenzied pitch. He may not have fully understood her need tonight, but he could see it, sense it. She leaned into it like the flower growing toward the sun. He grabbed her hair, a fistful on each side of her head like reins, and yanked each time he thrust.

"Jonathan, can I . . ." Her breathlessness coalesced into a long moan that set him afire.

"Come," he growled. One word was all he could manage before she screamed, clutching the sheets in her fists as swells of their fused hunger rose and crashed as one.

9

EMERGENCY CONTACT

At Octavia's desk, she paid the last of the bills and scheduled the DMs for the next few days so Octavia, due back at the end of the week, wouldn't have to.

Please—no more delays.

It wasn't the club that weighed on her; it was Charles's comment by the bar cart in Jonathan's apartment. *I trust we'll both keep each other's confidences.*

She could not do that for long. That night she had, perhaps selfishly, let Jonathan distract her. But Charles's words had troubled her, and he was the only person she could address it with. Unfortunately, she had not seen him since that night.

Jonathan offhandedly mentioned Charles was traveling for a few days and busy working on another deal, which might explain his absence from the club.

She had been so very close to telling Jonathan she had met Charles at Octavia's, but then she thought of the rules. She had an obligation to maintain confidentiality. Octavia would be incredibly disappointed if Quinn violated that.

She might revoke Quinn's membership or, worse, her friendship.

At the same time, she couldn't continue to ignore the elephant in the room that was her and Jonathan's relationship. Especially after the intensity, the closeness, of that night. She had been on the verge of telling him she loved him as they made love at dawn, her body aching everywhere from the previous evening, his touch so gentle, so loving and tender, it had nearly brought tears to her eyes.

But if Charles were keeping his club membership a secret—from Jonathan and, *please not*, from Becca—and Quinn knew about it, that would mean she was keeping the secret from them as well.

And that was not, to put it mildly, sustainable.

But there was always another perspective; she had learned that from writing fiction, if not from life itself. Maybe she was overthinking. Maybe one simple conversation with Charles would clarify everything. He might tell her it was fine if Jonathan knew. He might tell her that Becca, even if she didn't go to the club herself, was good with it.

Yes, maybe that's exactly how the conversation would go.

She looked through the old wedding text threads on her phone for Charles's number, but she didn't have it.

On Octavia's desktop computer, she opened the membership database and typed "Maximillian" into the search field.

When his record came up, Quinn glanced at the screen. His "connections" field was empty, as was the space for his emergency contact. At least on this screen, it was as if Becca didn't exist for Maximillian at all.

She scribbled his number on a sticky note and tapped out a text on her phone, saying they needed to talk.

Is it urgent?

She pictured one of his eyebrows rising as he read.

Yes, it is.

Monday at 11?

Monday? That was *days* away. And, right. Of course. Monday was her date day with Jonathan, the one he had asked her for, and she had agreed to, at the wedding. The day that was so important to him he had mentioned it excitedly several times. The day she should not reschedule for a reason she could not tell him.

Is that really the soonest you can talk?

Yes. I'll meet you there.

He wasn't using the club name. Her stomach churned.

She slid her phone into the back pocket of her black jeans and left Octavia's office.

On the main floor, she straightened up the rooms that had been used last night. The DMs left clean supplies and equipment on the counters to be put away today, each room, each drawer, each closet organized the same way to make it easy for members to find and keep track of things.

Nipple clamps, red and black ball gags, straps, harnesses, switches, paddles. She thought of bringing a few items to Jonathan for their play day, but she knew him—he would assume she was gently prompting him to do more, although that couldn't be farther from the truth. He might not consider himself a real dominant, but he was perfect for her.

Her phone vibrated and she yanked it out of her pocket. It had to be Charles, texting back with an earlier meeting day and time. Surely, he wanted to clear this up as quickly as she did.

She sighed and shook her head at the universe. It was Becca.

> Short notice, but are you by any chance in the city for a quick bite? My lunch meeting was canceled, and I've been wanting to talk to you.

Oh, thank goodness. Quinn let out a deep, tense breath as relief flooded her every pore. Becca did know. She was so sweet and thoughtful, she would want to tell Quinn she knew all about her and Charles meeting at the club. "We didn't want it to be weird," she would say. "But it's all good and, don't worry, I won't tell my mom."

> Yes, I'm in the city! Love to meet you. Name the time and place.

THE RESTAURANT CAME into view as soon as she turned the corner.

When she approached, a gust of wind caught the heavy wood door as she tugged on the sculpted brass handle, blowing it wide open.

Inside, the hostess was leading Becca to a table. Quinn hurried to catch up.

Once the woman left their menus, Becca turned to hug

Quinn. "I'm so glad this worked out. What are you up to in the city today?"

"Not much, really. I was . . . at Jonathan's and then . . . I was at . . ."

What if she was wrong about why Becca asked her to lunch?

For some reason, she thought of the bookshelves in Octavia's office. ". . . the library."

"Well, you look great," Becca said. "You have that rosy, I'm-in-love glow about you." She gestured around her face.

Quinn pictured last night, how Jonathan had held her and caressed her after he caned her, tickled her with the feather, pulled her hair as they shattered together. Her cheeks heated like glowing embers, and she looked away from Becca's happy, eager gaze. "Aww, thanks," she said. "He's wonderful; it's going well."

"As my mom would say, he's such a peach."

Quinn laughed at that. It was definitely something Leigh would say. "He *is* a peach," Quinn said, shifting in her seat to take the pressure off the sorest part of her rear.

A server came to their table, ran through the dishes on the blackboard, and took their order—an iced tea for herself and lemonade for Becca, along with two of the day's specials.

"Not to change the subject too abruptly, but I have something I'd like to ask you," Becca said. "But you have to promise me you'll give me an honest answer."

"I do, I will." Quinn bit the inside of her cheek. *Have you seen my new husband at your BDSM club?*

"It's actually a huge favor," Becca continued. "It's fine to say no."

"Ask away."

"I know you must still be recuperating from all the

wedding planning and the reception, but I was wondering— would you be willing to help me plan a shower?"

Okay, not what she was expecting. Or hoping.

"Of course I'll help. Is Robin getting married? Or Ji?" Robin was a childhood friend; Ji, her college roommate.

Becca giggled. "No, I mean a *baby* shower. For me—us. We're pregnant!"

Quinn coughed and took a drink from the slender straw in her tea. "My. That's . . . wonderful news." As a teenager, Becca had had some medical issues. It was hard in the moment to recall the details, but Quinn did remember Leigh saying pregnancy might not be an option. "I'm thrilled for you—that's incredible."

"But here's the thing," Becca went on. "Charles doesn't know yet. With my history, I want to wait to tell him until I know more. I have an appointment with my doctor next week. Mom's coming with me. In case we bump into each other between now and then, please don't say anything. And I hate to ask you to keep a secret from Jonathan, but can you not tell him either, so he doesn't slip with Charles?"

"I won't say anything, honey. It's your news to share."

Quinn excused herself to the restroom but continued past it to the side entrance of the restaurant.

Outside in the fresh air, she took a huge breath. Had she been breathing at all at the table? It didn't feel like it. Her lungs, her chest, they felt tight and empty.

Too many secrets.

If Becca was aware that Quinn and Charles both belonged to the club, she would have blurted it out the moment they sat down, that's how she was.

Charles's comment, his paltry record in Octavia's database, the leaden feeling in Quinn's gut right now—they all told her the truth, a truth she could no longer deny.

Becca did not know about Charles. Or that Quinn did.

With each day the stakes would rise: Jonathan's trust, Becca's, and—if Quinn told either of them about Charles—his and Octavia's and the club membership's trust in her as well.

Becca would be devastated. Charles would be furious. Their marriage would be at risk. Jonathan would feel betrayed Quinn hadn't confided in him, and he would not be able to abide that. The longer this went on, the worse the outcome would be.

That's how secrets were—at some point, they spun out and you lost all control.

10

A MEMBER ISSUE

He aimed for casual and not nervous.

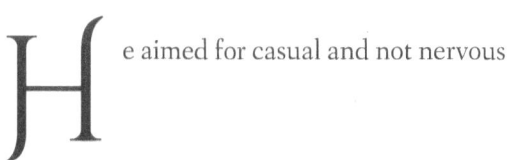

Missed you last night. Where are you?

It was Monday morning, and he was having breakfast at the cafe around the corner, one eye on his phone screen, the other on the business plan open on his laptop. He had been awake since five, getting ready for his play day with Quinn. He blew out a breath. *Dude, relax.*

He glanced at the time again. It wasn't even nine o'clock. She had told him she would be late, that she couldn't come over until noon, some member issue to deal with. This had not made him happy, but . . . okay, not that big a deal. They had gotten so much closer these past weeks, which made their play more meaningful.

Or was it the other way around?

Either way, a couple of hours was okay. He could chill,

work on his plan—his business plan; he already had a plan for her—and wait, semi-patiently, until noon.

He watched his phone for the three scrolling bubbles.

The blinking ellipsis soon appeared, then a message. He put down his fork and opened the text.

> On the train. Missed you too, but at least I got a full night's sleep. ;)

> That is a crying shame.

He added the crying-face emoji; she sent a laughing emoji back.

She had insisted on staying at the farmhouse last night. His place was a lot more convenient to the club than hers, so his guess was that she had needed time alone. Their nights lately had been pretty intense. Boundaries had been pushed —for both of them.

If she needed space now and then, he would give her space.

Besides, it had given him time to put the finishing touches on his improvised guest-room dungeon.

Damn if it didn't look like the real thing—at least what he knew of the real thing from the glimpse he caught that embarrassing night he had gone to Octavia's to find Quinn.

He had covered the white guest-room walls in black fabric for effect, except the wall to which he attached two long shelves for toys and hooks to hang his recently acquired selection of floggers and paddles and restraints. It wasn't a huge room but, still, a St. Andrew's cross, spanking bench, bondage chair—somehow they all fit, and he could not wait to show her.

Although she would be blindfolded at first. He had the

day choreographed. Thank you, internet, for technique videos and inspiration.

But now that everything was in place, he vowed to be productive for the next three hours. He would not let thoughts of her, or what he planned to do with her, eat up the time.

He had work to do.

But he could not resist.

> Touch yourself and send me a picture.

Eww! On. The. Train.

> Disobeying?

No, Jonathan. But please wait til I get to the club.

She added the batting eyelashes emoji.

> Okay, but now you have to send me two photos, one of you touching and one of you coming.

> . . .

> Make that one a video.

I'll try. But I have things to do and then that meeting.

> ARE you disobeying? It's sounding that way.

No. Jonathan.

Then I'll be waiting.

He set the phone on the table face down but turned up the volume so he wouldn't miss the chime of her text.

Two texts actually, one with a video. Of her coming. He shifted the napkin in his lap to cover the anticipatory movement in his pants.

Get back to work.

The spreadsheet of financial projections on his laptop grew fuzzy and meaningless, as if his thoughts of her doing what he just asked blurred his vision. All those rows and columns and numbers.

He packed up while he waited for the check and then headed toward home. In this state, he would work better there.

The phone chimed as he neared his building, but he ignored it. That's all he would need—some stray paparazzo snapping a shot of him with a lascivious look on his face and a burgeoning hard-on in his pants. He could imagine the hashtags now.

Inside, safely ensconced in his elevator, he opened the message and tapped the image to make it bigger.

He would Never. Ever. Tire. of looking at that.

The purple handle of a toy was visible in the photo—visible but blurry. The rest of the shot was in focus, which meant it was vibrating.

He dropped his bag in the entry gallery, glanced at the glass door wall across the living room, and headed in the opposite direction, into the windowless powder room to unzip his pants.

He got harder looking at the image again, imagining he was playing with her, drifting the toy in and out, pausing at her entrance to drive her mad, sending it back inside until her neck arched and she moaned and . . .

Wait, she was still going to send a video. *99 . . . 98 . . . Cool your jets, man. 92 . . .*

He turned on the tap, leaned his head over the sink, splashed cold water on his face.

His phone chimed.

> The video you requested. Jonathan.

He hit the play arrow, left the phone on the counter, and took hold of himself.

The video provided confirmation—the toy was definitely vibrating. She moved it slowly, just as he imagined a few seconds ago, arched her hips, let out a quiet whimper.

He pictured her in Octavia's office, the door locked, careful to be quiet so no one would hear.

He stopped it and replayed those few seconds, the rocking hips, the breathy mewl of need and loss of control, that split second of free fall at the start of her orgasm when there was no turning back, no holding on, only letting go.

He loved that moment. He would never stop loving that moment.

His own movements sped up as she moaned quiet as a mouse, and he watched her lips convulse around the toy. *Damn, Quinn.* The thought of her like that, it made him tremble as his climax followed hers.

He took a minute to recover, leaning against the wall. She wasn't the send dirty videos type, but with him, she just had.

Another layer peeled away, bringing them closer. He cleaned up and picked up his phone.

> Hot. So very hot.

How hot? ;)

> That hot.

He was grinning like a fool. She knew him as well as he knew her.

Glad you liked it. Gotta go to work.

> Getting the spiked paddles and handcuffs ready?

She sent him the emoji with the lips zipped shut.

> Teasing. I know you can't say.

Okay, now he would get back to work. She was busy, and the pressure that had been building in him all morning had been released.

His spreadsheet was clearer now, and he filled in the cells with the missing figures, calculating additional profit projections for conservative, middle of the road, and wildly optimistic scenarios in the first year.

He held his breath as he filled in the numbers for years two and three.

Dare he put such hopeful possibilities out there?

His answer to that question, finally, was yes. In large part because he imagined sharing those figures with Quinn, imagined how proud he would be to show her Jaines Productions was killing it.

11

SINGLE, SIMPLE TRUTH

A t least the club was empty, so there was no one for her to disturb with her nervous energy. She paced, walked up and down the staircases, from the entry level up to Octavia's office on the fifth floor, down, and back up again.

The tension pulled her taut, a rubber band ready to snap. Maybe not the most original analogy, but it captured how she felt. She wasn't outright lying to Jonathan, but she wasn't telling him the whole truth, either.

A member issue.

That, it was. Charles was a member. But that Quinn had seen him here without Becca, and with someone else— someone else whom, more and more, Becca didn't seem to be aware of—those were all things Jonathan would expect her to share with him rather than omit.

And yet.

As she plodded up the stairs again, heartbeat pounding in her ears, she reviewed the plan for her conversation with Charles. Especially after learning Becca was pregnant, it was clear Quinn needed to convince him to come clean to his wife about his membership at Octavia's. And to give his consent for Quinn to tell Jonathan the two of them had bumped into each other here.

And her backup plan if he wouldn't agree? Ask him to stop coming to the club until Octavia returned from France and Quinn could be the one to make herself scarce. It wouldn't change the fact of Quinn's knowing, but at least she wouldn't be privy to the everyday details, like, say, for example, that he had been at the club right before that dinner at Jonathan's last week. Or, that he scened, more than once, with that naked woman with the knots and collar.

If it weren't right there in her face, if Quinn no longer came to the club, perhaps she could at least have plausible deniability.

But who was she kidding?

She had seen what she had seen; there was no putting the mask back on Maximillian.

And now there was only one solution: Becca needed to know the truth and, despite Quinn's growing desire to tell her herself, immediately—which came with its own set of disasters—Charles needed to be the one to deliver the news.

Rather, there were two solutions: Quinn also needed to tell Jonathan about the unexpected connection at Octavia's that touched all four of their lives.

On the main level, she checked the clock on the wall. 10:47. Thirteen minutes to go. She could make it back up to the fifth floor, get her things, turn off Octavia's computer, and get back down here right before eleven. That way, she could be out the door the second she and Charles were through talking and get to Jonathan's a.s.a.p.

Her phone chimed as she was huffing past the fourth floor.

> I need to push our meeting to 1:15.

Oh, no, no, no.

She really didn't understand. He seemed like a genuinely sweet, caring guy when he was with Becca, but here he acted as if he were a completely different person.

And not one Quinn liked very much.

> Charles. This is important. And I have an appointment to get to. Is there ANY way you can make it earlier? Please.

It might sound like she was begging, but so be it. Apparently, surprisingly, he had trouble grasping the seriousness of their situation.

> 1:15.

Quickly, she texted Jonathan.

> Unfortunately, the meeting got delayed and I'll be late, but I should be there by 2:30. Sorry!!!

The three bubbles lit and faded, lit and faded, then stopped without a message appearing.

Again they started, and again they stopped.

She absolutely hated this. She wanted to tell him everything. Everything. Including how, underneath all of this was a single, simple truth. She loved him.

Especially the last time they were together—the most

intense and exquisite connection—the words had been perched on the tip of her tongue.

But she could not in good conscience tell him now. Not until there was a resolution with Charles. So that nothing— no lie or half-truth or omitted information about people he cared about and, now, worked with—stood between them.

───────

HE PACED. And paced. And paced some more, hoping on one of these trips across his guest room that the looming headache would go away.

He tried to be understanding when she told him she had to schedule something this morning and wouldn't arrive until noon. That was bad enough. But then she texted again a little while ago to say she wouldn't be here until closer to three, all because some club member couldn't meet with her any earlier.

This wasn't the full day together he had planned. Trying to suppress his irritation, he reminded himself she was, after all, coming to see him, and that she was taking this club thing seriously, trying to mediate an issue between members so she could fulfill her promise to Octavia.

He loved this about her, her loyalty.

Loved and, right now, hated. The logical part of his brain understood her commitment, but the rest of him, brain and wood alike, throbbed with the need for her to be here.

Now.

As he walked by the new shelves he had installed, he saw the nipple clamps he had placed there earlier. Besides blindfolding her first thing and tying her hands behind her back with a silk scarf, he would take the clamps for a spin too.

And then he would order her to her knees to take him in her mouth. With her hands tied, he would hold her head and guide her movements, snaking his fingers in her hair to release that familiar scent. The clamps would tug on her, heightening the sensation, amplifying her pleasure. He would not last long watching this, reveling in her warm mouth. But once he came, he would take his time with her the rest of the afternoon. He would tease her and bring her back from the edge. Over and over and over, until she asked —begged—to come.

Please, Jonathan. Hearing her say his name as she moaned with pleasure was right up there for him with the scent of her hair. The only fixed point they had for what remained of the day was the rescheduled dinner reservation at Vieve at eight, for a private booth with drapes and a call button for the wait staff so you could dine—or, feast as it were—without interruption.

Which was exactly what he planned to do.

Their public play was fast becoming a fetish of his. With Quinn, he got off on the contrast—such intimate physical acts out in the open that brought them closer, each encounter a shared secret.

It might last only a few minutes, but in those moments, no matter where they were or what was going on around them, there was extraordinary trust on her part and responsibility on his not to let them get caught. In those moments, it was just the two of them, the two of them sharing the most incredible intimacy.

When he heard the sound of an incoming text, he grabbed his phone. Maybe the member canceled and she was on her way.

Do you happen to know where Charles is?

He looked at the number. It wasn't Quinn; it was Leigh.

> No. Texted him earlier but haven't heard back. Everything ok?

Becca hospital.

> Where? What happened?

NY General. Explain later. Need to find C.

> I'll tell Quinn. She's

> . . .

He hesitated. He couldn't very well write that she was at Octavia's.

> at a meeting. We'll meet you at hosp.

Then he tapped out a message to let Quinn know.

> Emergency. Becca's at NY General. Come to the apt, and we'll go together?

He watched the second hand click around the clock for five minutes that dragged like three hours.

No answer. Maybe she was still meeting with that member.

Screw it.

He would break his rule about staying away from the club. It was closed today anyway, which made it less of a risk. But, whatever. Didn't matter. This was important; he needed to go get her.

THE DRESSING ROOM door opened onto the main floor at precisely one fifteen. Quinn got up from the couch in one of the alcoves where she had been waiting, her bag and coat beside her so she could dash as soon as she and Charles were done talking. When she looked up toward him, he was wearing his usual mask. "Kayla."

Oh, please.

"Charles." She would not call him by his club name, a not-so-subtle way of reminding him she was fully aware of his identity. "It's just me; no one else is here," she told him. "You don't have to wear the mask."

He looked around like he might not believe her, but then slowly reached up and slid it off. "So then. To what do I owe the pleasure?" he asked as they stood on the open, empty floor.

She wanted to tell him what he could do with his snark —and the bogus accent. Instead, she said, "You know why we're here, Charles."

"Kayla. You look a bit . . . rattled. Is playing dress-up domina not so easy? A bit more to it than finding something —but nothing too revealing—in Octavia's closet?" He was using the accent inconsistently; maybe he was rattled, too.

"This isn't about me."

He laughed, a snorting, mocking kind of laugh, not what she would have expected from the Charles she knew as Becca's husband. "I'm going to guess that, in fact, this is *all* about you. So tell me, what is so incredibly urgent?"

Ignore the sarcasm. She had to stay focused on her goal.

"Is Becca aware that you're a member here?"

"Kayla. That is absolutely none of your business."

"Okay, let me rephrase the question. From things you've said, I can only assume Becca does not know you're a member. But she needs to."

"I beg your pardon. What she needs is also none of your business," he answered.

She was really, *really* disliking this version of him. So much so, she wanted him to put his mask back on.

"This is where you're wrong, Charles, where your 'We'll just mind our own business and pretend we don't know the other is here' approach breaks down. Becca is my business, too. As is Jonathan. Both of them would be destroyed if they discovered we were keeping this kind of secret from them. And it's only a matter of time until that discovery."

His head jerked. "Is that a threat?"

"It's not meant to be a threat, no. But I can't keep your double life from the two of them. I'm asking you—begging you—to tell her, and also to let me tell Jonathan. Please, Charles. We have too many connections. Especially now that you're investing in his company—you've bound the four of us even closer."

He smirked. "Interesting word choice. But that's neither here nor there. I invested because Jonathan has a compelling business idea and he's one of the few people with the personality, talent, and connections to pull it off." He paced a few steps away, then turned on his heel back toward her, hands on his hips. "But that any of this—my business decisions, my personal life—has to do with you . . . How you put yourself in the center of the universe is absolutely amazing."

Her chest squeezed so tight, it was hard to take the breath she needed.

"You're right, Charles—what you do is none of my business. *Except* where it intersects my life. *Except* that I know something about you that the people you and I are closest to —including your *wife*—do not. And I, we, can't be a party to your deception."

"Just who do you mean by 'we'?"

"Jonathan and me."

He cocked an eyebrow. "So you're speaking for him?"

"Of course not. But if he knew you were lying to Becca, he would say the same thing."

He scoffed and shook his head, his eyes widening. "Would he, now?"

"As a member, I need to keep your information confidential, but by doing that I'm betraying *everyone* in our lives. All I'm asking is for you to . . ."

"I'm aware of what you've asked"—he cut her off—"and my answer is no. What I can do is pull my promised investment if that helps loosen our ties and ease your Girl Scout conscience. Would you like that?"

What? She just stared at him. Their web of friendship and secrets and, as a result, lies, was tangling by the second.

And then she realized what she was feeling—the sense of a subtle shift, the certainty that it would set off the avalanche, that something stable was about to give way.

"Seriously, Kayla? You would ask me to pull my investment from your partner's project?" Now he was the one staring in disbelief and, she realized, he had not used his fake accent in a while.

His face, his expression, changed from the confident, arrogant countenance of Maximillian to something else.

Pain? And the averted gaze, his pressed lips, the angled downward tilt of his head. Shame?

Perhaps she had finally reached the real man. The man who must have very powerful reasons for deceiving the woman he loved, and likely many other people as well. What had happened to him to make him do this? If she were writing him as a character in a novel, that was the question she would explore. There was an anguished story there, of that she was now sure.

He inhaled to speak just as his phone sounded from inside his suit jacket—a few notes from the opening theme of Jonathan's show. She could easily identify those notes; she had binged episode after episode, a continuous stream of him over the summer when they were out of touch.

"Speak of the devil," Charles said, taking out the phone, his index finger hovering over the green answer icon. "Now is your opportunity, Kayla. I can tell him Demeleo Investment Group is backing out. I'm sure he would prefer to know sooner rather than later." His glower dared her. "What will it be?"

"No, no. Don't back out. Don't pull your investment," she stammered.

She pictured the spark in Jonathan's eyes when he talked about getting to work on his own shows, for his own company. She was so proud of him for taking a risk, for not waiting for a network to offer him something but to take charge of his career and do what he dreamed of. All the traits that made him successful—his talent, his intelligence, his curiosity, his way with people, his openness to new experiences—also made him a wonderful friend and partner, not to mention an incredibly passionate, creative lover.

She would let him go before she took this opportunity away from him.

"I thought you might say that. My advice to you then, Kayla, is to stay in your lane, especially where Becca and I are concerned. Go to another club if you want distance, but stop judging and second-guessing what I do."

And with that, he tapped the screen to answer Jonathan's call, but it had already gone to voicemail.

JONATHAN HUNG up at the too-familiar start of Charles's voicemail. He continued to wait across the street from Octavia's for a few more beats, gazing at a shop window so he could scan the surrounding area in the reflection. Today every jackass with a smart phone was a risk.

Being caught at Octavia's would be hard to explain to Charles. And if he told Charles he was there to pick up Quinn, well, then he was outing her.

But maybe his dilemma was solved. A narrow door underneath the club's regal front staircase opened.

It wasn't Quinn, but a tall guy in a long coat, turning back as if to say one last thing to whoever he was talking to inside. But then he emerged from the club, his stride familiar as he hurried toward the street, his arm raised to hail a cab.

No fucking way. Charles.

And the woman behind him, rushing to catch up, who put her hand on his back as soon as she reached him? Jonathan felt sucker-punched, a left hook to the gut.

Quinn.

The two of them stood together at the curb. They finally must have seen their messages, because they both wore worried expressions.

A taxi pulled up and they got in, oblivious to Jonathan's

presence. When it squealed away, he crossed the street and hailed his own cab.

"New York General. As fast as you can, please." He pulled the door closed and fell back against the vinyl seat.

Quinn and Charles.

Jonathan's Quinn and Charles who just married Becca. At a dungeon. Was this really happening?

His phone vibrated in his jacket pocket and his hand felt heavy as he reached for it, like he was moving through water. A text from her slid across his screen.

> Don't wait for me. Meet you at hospital.

As the cab neared the building, he asked the driver to hang back until the two of them got out of their car in front of him. Charles jogged to the hospital doors, while Quinn stayed out front and looked at her phone, then typed something.

His phone signaled another text. It was her.

> I'm here.

The urge to turn around and go back to his apartment, or anywhere else but here, was so strong, it forced his fingers into a tight fist.

But he had to make sure Becca was okay and to be there for Leigh. He also had to see what kind of bullshit story Quinn and Charles were going to feed him.

Quinn and Charles. At Octavia's.

He typed back furiously.

> I or We?????!!!

. . .

Don't make assumptions

. . .

Where are you?

It began to make sense—the tension he sensed in her recently, missing half of their date day. Man. He was such an idiot, and karma was a bitch. Didn't he deserve this, to be cheated on? To have the other shoe drop just as he started to believe that things might work out—with Quinn, with his new venture, with Charles as an investor?

Damn it. He felt so fucking, fucking stupid. Their relationship had seemed so strong, so close, so solid—so much so that he had quelled the voices of the devilish assholes on his shoulder, whispering that what he did for her, to her, wouldn't be enough. He had upped his game—yanked her hair hard, caned her ass until welts rose, made her come again and again and again, fucked her with a plug inside her, outfitted his spare room as a goddamn dungeon.

But apparently he had been right. It, he, was not enough. That familiar sense of inadequacy reared. She needed more, and she had gone elsewhere—not just to the club but to someone else. Of all people, to Charles.

What a great effing judge of character he was—of Quinn and of Charles, too.

When the light changed, he stormed across the street straight toward her. "So *he* was the big important issue?"

"Jonathan, let me explain. It's not what you think."

It's not what you think.

Hadn't he said the exact same thing to Delphine? Only

"it" was exactly what she thought, and he had lied through his teeth that it wasn't.

"Oh? It wasn't you? At Octavia's? With Charles?"

She held his gaze, steady. "Yes, it was all of that, but . . ."

He thought of the times they had gotten together as a foursome the last couple of weeks. He didn't want to hear her excuses. "How long has it been going on?" he interrupted.

"We have not been having a . . . relationship, an affair, if that's what you're implying."

"Well then, let me be more precise for the wordsmith. How long have you been going to the club together?"

As if that didn't count as an affair.

She shook her head at him. "We have not been going to the club together. We have not done anything together. I asked him if we could talk, and today was the only day he was available. He met me at the club a little while ago to have that conversation."

He was pacing again, back and forth only a few feet in front of the woman he thought he was in love with, the one he thought he knew. Inside and out.

How could he have missed this?

He so wanted to believe it wasn't true, that she hadn't been lying, that she hadn't cheated on him. But that still left the matter of her and Charles at Octavia's.

"Just the fact that you two were meeting at Octavia's and not mentioning it and not answering your phones when people were trying to reach you about Becca, who's lying in a hospital bed, *not* playing at the club with you and her husband . . . What do you call that?" People were watching them, but he did not care. "Because to me, it sounds a lot like cheating."

"How dare you." Her hands tensed at her sides. "Don't

project your guilty conscience onto me," she spat, lips and skin tight around her mouth. "I, we, did not cheat. I realized at the wedding reception that I had seen him at the club, but he always wore a mask. A full face mask. He has a scar on his arm. That's what I recognized when he made that bonfire with his friends and I brought them marshmallows, alright?"

Her eyes blazed. "At first, I assumed Becca must know he went to the club but as time went on, it became clear she didn't. You know I can't talk about members, but I also couldn't keep his secret from Becca and especially from you. That's why I arranged to talk to him today, to try to reason with him, to get him to tell Becca—and let him know I had to tell you."

Was she seriously handing him this crock of shit?

"So you knew—since he *married* Becca—that he was a member at Octavia's, and you didn't think you should have *mentioned* it to me right away? Let alone to his *wife*?" His voice was loud now, and she led him to a quieter spot away from the people lingering near the hospital entrance, smoking, pacing, waiting for news.

"You know why I couldn't tell you. You or Becca." Her voice quieted, but he was not near done.

"You chose to protect Charles over Becca, and over me. What am I supposed to do with that?"

"I had, have, an obligation to the community—"

"Oh, save the bullshit, Quinn! Obligation to The Community, my ass. Becca is not The Community. I am not The Community." He wiped a spray of wayward spit from the side of his mouth. "You should have told Becca. And you should have told me!"

She jabbed her index finger toward his chest, her eyes once again fiery. "Don't be so self-righteous—"

He jerked back while shoving her hand away. "It's not that, it's—"

"It's that *you* would have gone to Becca and told her," she interrupted. "For what? So you could redeem yourself? So you could use their situation to make up for your lack of honesty, your ruined marriage? They're *happy* together."

His mind flashed to Delphine. "How can she be happy when she doesn't know what he's doing behind her back?"

"You and I might not like that she doesn't know he belongs to Octavia's, but it's not our place to tell her. Especially now."

Her voice slowed, like she caught herself about to say something she didn't want to. How had he not noticed this before, the withholding?

"Becca is going to need support from us," she went on, "not you tearing her life apart with information that isn't yours, or mine, to divulge."

She spoke as if she knew what was happening with Becca.

"Is she okay—why is she here?" he asked Quinn, pointing toward the building.

"She's pregnant. But she's had trouble in the past, so I hope she still is."

He felt his eyes widen. "How long have you known?"

"A few days. She told me in confidence and asked me not to tell you until she told Charles. Which she hasn't yet. She was waiting until after her next doctor's appointment this week to surprise him."

She took a step away from him toward the hospital doors. "We've all kept secrets, Jonathan. Some potentially more dangerous than others, but secrets nonetheless. I am truly sorry I didn't tell you about Charles, but I couldn't. I hope you can . . ." She reached for his hand, but he shoved it away again, bewildered by all of this.

There was no way he was going through those doors with her or standing around Becca's bed while he watched Charles lie to his wife.

Instead, he would call Becca later. Right now he was not going to participate in this clusterfuck, thank you very much.

As he turned to leave, he had only one thing left to say. "I thought I knew you, Quinn, but I realize now I don't have any clue who you are."

12

___

IGNORE

His words cut like a dull blade, ragged, deep, and aching. How he knew her, from that very first night when she somehow had found the boldness to send his driver away, was the most precious thing between them. To hear him say she was a stranger to him? She didn't dare watch him walk away. Instead, she sat at the end of the bench by the sliding doors; she felt like if she didn't, she might actually lose her balance.

But even hearing him say those words didn't hurt as much as seeing the shock and betrayal on his face when he crossed the street toward her. Of course he assumed she was cheating; from his perspective, it all pointed to that. And although she had good reasons, she *had* betrayed his trust. He expected, as had she, that there were no secrets between them.

For a man who had once betrayed his partner's trust, for a man who never would fully forgive himself for what he did, trust was everything.

Everything.

Sadness tugged, and she rubbed her chest absentmindedly. He would be the last man she would ever let herself love like this, and she hated that she hadn't gotten the chance to tell him how she felt. Their relationship would end with him feeling deceived and discounted, not adored and understood the way he had, until a few moments ago, adored and understood her.

She would have to live with that, the saddest truth of all.

A pigeon squawked at a man sitting on another bench nearby, his eyes vacant with grief. Her sadness would have to wait; she was here because of Becca. Although she should prepare herself to lose Becca, too.

Quinn's life was different than before. *She* was different than before. Not everyone would accept her now.

Harris was gone. Octavia, her friendship, and her club had shown Quinn an unfamiliar world, one she was now a part of, and that world came with a code of conduct.

Quinn had choices to make about how she would live the rest of her life because the old one was gone; she could not go back.

At the reception desk inside the hospital lobby, she got directions to Becca's room and took the elevator to the eighth floor. The doors opened and she turned left, as instructed. As she continued down the long corridor, Leigh came out of one of the rooms. Quinn sped up, and Leigh turned just as she caught up.

"How is she?" Quinn blurted.

"She's okay." Leigh's eyes glistened with relief. "And the doctor thinks she should still be able to have a healthy pregnancy."

"Oh, thank goodness." Quinn reached for Leigh and held her.

"She'll be on bedrest for a few weeks, and the doctor's going to watch her like a hawk, but she's okay." Quinn held onto her as she spoke, Leigh's exhaustion and relief palpable. "Where's Jonathan?" she asked. "He said he was picking you up from a meeting or something?"

Yeah, something. "He, um . . . I think he's going to come back later."

"Oh." Leigh looked puzzled. If she weren't so flustered, she would have asked Quinn a lot more questions. "You look . . . worn out. Is everything okay?"

"Everything's fine," she flat-out lied.

"Okay, good. Let's have a nice, long catch-up once Becca's home and settled."

"Yes, let's." *If you're still speaking to me.*

"Now that Charles is here with Becca, I'm going to grab a *real* cup of coffee. Come with?"

"You go. I'll just poke my head in for a minute to see her."

She watched Leigh leave, high heels tapping down the hall to the elevators. A prick of sadness pierced Quinn's chest at the close friendship they once had, the old friendship in which Leigh knew nearly everything about her. That Quinn was a member of Octavia's would melt Leigh's eyebrows. Even if Leigh didn't say it, she would think the same thing Jonathan did: *I don't know who you are.*

Rustling behind her interrupted her thoughts, and she turned back toward the doorway Leigh had come from.

Charles was leaving the room, looking—it was hard to decipher what she saw—relieved, fearful, joyful, guilty? But maybe she saw in his expression what she expected to see. This was Maximillian, and he was good at hiding in plain sight.

Hiding and disguising himself. Again, she felt that mix of sympathy and empathy, and she reached out to touch his forearm. "It sounds like things will be fine," she said. "That's wonderful news."

He nodded, then just looked at her. She hated that she couldn't see behind the wall.

"Congratulations—you're going to be a dad." She rubbed his arm as if that could jostle him into expressing some emotion.

Wait . . . progress. His eyes sparked. "It's incredible," he said, nodding. "Unexpected but incredible."

"It is. I'm happy for you. Both of you."

His demeanor softened. "I suppose life will change."

She wondered if he was referring to the club. "Life is always changing." She shifted her weight and whispered. "Do you really believe it's none of my business, Charles? Or that no one would have found out?"

He held her gaze. A silent command to quit with the questions, or a crack in the armor? She went with option B and kept at him, this time in a gentler voice. "Why can't you tell her? I mean, not while she's here, but once she's home? Can't you?"

"Kayla." He exhaled, the shake of his head indicating she was missing the point. "We're not so different, you and me. The need to reinvent ourselves, the . . . curse . . . of finding something so perfect, so sublime, the one thing that fits us like a glove. And yet. It forces choices we wouldn't otherwise make to protect ourselves and the people we love from who we've become."

"But Becca is your partner. She . . ."

"I'm aware of my relationship to Becca. Perhaps someday I'll share my reinvention story with you, and we can sing Kumbaya together and lick sticky marshmallow off our fingers."

Okay, so the softening stopped and Maximillian's

sarcasm was back. "But not before I tell it to—as you continue to so-helpfully remind me—my wife. And before you ask me for a timetable, I don't know when that will be."

Underneath the defensive tone it was clearer and clearer to her that a man who had been exposed, shamed, lurked beneath. She wouldn't push him more; he might one day trust her with his story, and he might not. No matter what, he would have to trust Becca with it first; that would be an immense step.

"Well, she's okay—that's the most important thing."

He nodded and blew out a breath. "You might have intruded on my life but, Quinn, I *have* heard what you've said—and I appreciate how much you care about Becca."

Quinn, not Kayla.

"That I do," she said. But although Becca was the reason she was here, this conversation happening a couple of feet from her door brought reality a bit too close for comfort.

Until Charles confided in his partner, Quinn would have to continue pretending their paths hadn't crossed at the club.

And she would have to withhold the truth when Becca and Leigh would no doubt ask why she and Jonathan had split up.

Because with that look in his eyes and what he said about not knowing who she was, he didn't need to say in so many words that they were through.

The tears would not stay back much longer, and she couldn't bring herself to lie to Becca like she had lied to Leigh a few moments ago. *Everything's fine.* "I'm leaving," she told Charles. "When you go back to her, please tell her I stopped by and I'll check on her another time."

JONATHAN WAITED across the street until she went inside the hospital, her hands stuffed in the pockets of her short black jacket. The hems of her black pants flared over shiny heels with pointy toes. Her look said smart, chic, business casual; no one else would know where she had just come from or what she had been doing.

You don't really even know, do you?

No, he didn't. But Charles did.

He began skulking toward the apartment. The walk would be good, because otherwise he would need to find a punching bag since in reality he would never actually hit Charles's well-groomed, two-faced face.

Better yet, he turned down the familiar alley to his favorite neighborhood hole-in-the-wall bar. It was one of the few places in the city he could go to think and hide at the same time. Like a close old friend you might not see often, but when you did, you picked up just like old times.

The vintage linoleum floor squeaked from stickiness as he neared the bar, his eyes slowly adjusting to the dim light. "Hey, man," the bartender said. "Been a long time. Welcome back. You look like shit."

"Screw you, too, Derek." He reached out to shake his hand, then settled on a barstool and unzipped his jacket.

"Double neat?" Derek asked, already reaching for the bourbon.

Definitely a friend. "That's a good start." He glanced around. Other than a couple at a table in the dark back corner leaning in toward each other, oblivious to their surroundings, he was the only customer.

Derek set the glass on the bar in front of him. "I'm guessing you don't wanna talk about it?"

Jonathan raised the glass in a toasting gesture. "Not at all. Thanks, man."

"You got it." The bottle clinked against the crowded shelf as Derek put it back in the lineup.

Jonathan watched the couple. They were sitting next to each other on the same side of the booth. This place, that table, mid-day—it was a rendezvous, no doubt about it.

He was sure because he had been there. Not this place or that table, but in the same mid-day haunts. Hotel rooms, dark bars, first-class airport lounges, mini-airplane suites with fold-flat seats that qualified him several times over—what a point of pride—for the mile-high club.

We all have kept secrets, Jonathan. Some more dangerous than others.

Didn't Becca have a right to know the truth about the man she married? How could Quinn not see where her loyalty should lie? How could she not have told him? *Him.*

Actually, he had the answer to this last one. Because she knew he would have insisted she tell Becca, or he would have.

And then Quinn would have kicked him to the curb immediately, no questions asked. He picked at a nick in the glass rim with his thumbnail and stared into the amber liquid. Instead she kept it from him and, still, the outcome was the same—it was over between them. He would not be able to trust her again after this.

Somewhere between his second or fifth pour, a giggle from the corner table floated his way. Maybe it was his imagination messing with him, but it looked like the guy was getting a hand job under the table. Get a room.

Shit, that reminded him. He texted Vieve to cancel his reservation for the private booth tonight. This was the second time; last week he had canceled so he could have

Becca and Charles over for dinner instead. The memory came roaring back—dinner with the remote-controlled toy. They probably got a good laugh at that, Quinn and her club buddy. In on their own little secret together, Jonathan the outsider.

He would get over her. Eventually. And he would find a new investment partner. He didn't need Charles's hush money. Because that's what it was, wasn't it? Or was Charles's decision to invest because he felt guilty playing with Quinn behind Jonathan's back? Or was the money meant to keep Quinn accessible? When Jonathan had put the budget together for the business plan, he had earmarked a hefty sum for travel. For *weeks* at a time.

Busy and out of town. How nice for the two of them.

Derek set another drink on the bar. This one was lighter than the others. Yes, Jonathan had become that guy, the one who sits at the bar so long, the bartender diluted his drinks. "Can I get you something to eat? Burger?"

"Nah, I'm good, man. I can handle it. Lotta practice." He raised the glass again. "But thanks for the concern." Derek took a step back and wobbled sideways. Or maybe Jonathan was the one listing. *Shit.* "Okay, I hear you, man. Can I get a burger to go? And then I'll take my sorry ass home."

He stood slowly, peeled some bills from the cash in his wallet, and slid them across the bar. Derek slid a couple back to him. Now there was an honest guy. "Don't be a stranger." One of them wobbled past center to the other side. "Stop by once in a while, not only when life's in the shits—Tuesday night is trivia; Thursday night is poker."

Without Quinn, that's the promise his future evenings held, game night at the bar.

At least when he got outside, it was almost dark, no happy late-afternoon sunshine stabbing him in the eyes.

He crossed the street with the crowd at the corner and turned toward home.

He should go somewhere else, somewhere he wouldn't just lay on the couch and stew for the rest of the evening. But as big as this crazy city was, he couldn't think of one single place he wanted to be.

———

THE TRAIN CLATTERED NORTH from Grand Central as the conductor stopped beside Quinn, clicked her ticket in a mysterious pattern, and wedged it under the metal tab at the top of her seat.

Out the window, into the darkness, she watched the lights along the Hudson. You didn't have to be a writer to see the metaphor—away from Manhattan, away from the club, away from Jonathan.

By the time she got off at River Run Falls, the queasiness she'd felt all day settled in her body like a brick. Instead of taking one of the cabs waiting outside the station, she walked home, hoping the cool night air would quell it.

The wood floor creaked as she entered the house. She was still learning it, all its unfamiliar textures and scents and sounds. Between staying at Jonathan's and spending her days at the club, she hadn't been here much.

That would change. Now she would have more time to get to know this place. Octavia would be back in a few days, so Quinn wouldn't be needed at the club and, well . . . she probably would not be going to Jonathan's again.

A fresh wave of queasiness roiled.

Tea. She should make tea.

She set the kettle to boil and took the tin of loose tea from the back of the countertop, releasing the scent of jasmine. Its fragrance brought him into clear focus in her mind's eye, how he had made her tea the night she moved in, how he'd drawn her bath, how they had kissed for the first time. The memories only worsened the real physical ache in her chest. Was this how it was going to be, that everything here would remind her of him?

She spooned tea leaves into the infuser, poured the hot water into her mug, and carried it to the living room. On the couch, legs folded beneath her, she stared into the cold hearth, gray ash dusting the floor of the firebox. Carefully, she tried to sip the steaming liquid, but it was too hot to drink. She set the mug down and got her phone. Once he had a chance to calm down, to think about this rationally, he would talk to her. Of course he would.

Come on Jonathan. Pick up. Please. Pick. Up.

HE THREW his coat on the table in the entry and closed the shades in the living room to keep out the lights. So many lights. Bright lights. He sat on the couch, unwrapped the burger from Derek, and opened his laptop, squinting to find the key to lower the brightness.

Even dim, the screen wobbled like Derek had. Screw it. He adjusted the pillows and laid down instead.

When he opened his eyes, the blue numbers on the cable box read 8:21. Jesus, he had slept, what, three, four hours? His mouth tasted like . . . wallpaper paste. Not that he had ever tried wallpaper paste, but it was probably a close match.

He sat up carefully to assess the damage. A little dizzy.

A headache in the background. But, unfortunately, not enough of one to ward off his mind's replay of the day— from working on financial projections and getting nipple clamps ready for Quinn to watching her and Charles emerge together from Octavia's.

A bad dream. Only it wasn't.

Out of habit, he picked up the phone. A missed call from Leigh at 7:34 p.m. Her voicemail said Becca was going to stay the night in the hospital. They wanted to keep her for observation. How convenient for Charles. He could go to the club. Maybe Quinn would go with him.

The phone shook in his hand, and her number marched across the screen. Um, hard no. He was not ready to hear that voice.

Ignore.

She had told him that her and Charles's . . . whatever the hell it was . . . dated back to the wedding. Now that he thought about it, she had seemed shaken that night and, stupid him, he assumed it was the stress of trying to make every detail of the reception perfect. Or that she was thinking back to her own wedding and feeling blue. He understood that, anticipated it even, that's why he had reiterated how she could talk about Harris, how she shouldn't feel any pressure from Jonathan. He would be patient, he understood.

At the time, it had all struck him as very mature and adult, and she had been different with him after—closer, affectionate. She smiled more. Seeing that change in her had made him so freaking happy. What a fool he was.

And those times he made her come in a secret frenzy while others were right nearby? Each time as she dropped off the ledge, the look in her eyes gave him a sensation he couldn't put into words, like she was saying, pleading. *Send me. Protect me. Push me over, catch me when I fall.*

He had eaten it up, loved every nanosecond and molecule about it.

Idiot.

He got up and hauled his sorry ass to the kitchen to make coffee. While it brewed, he took a quick shower to clear his head and get rid of the *eau de fried bar food* stink that hung over him like a rain cloud. The coffee, the shower, they were a morning routine, and now his body clock would be upside down, but who gave a shit?

He could do what he wanted. He was independent, on his own, a free agent.

Alone.

On the way back to the kitchen, he stopped at the door to the spare room. The silk scarf on the bed, the nipple clamps, the flogger, the feather, the shelves full of toys.

He had been so clueless.

He picked up the cane. How much time had he spent watching online videos and reading books about proper technique to make sure he didn't hurt her or strike the wrong part of her body? And how many blog posts had he read to learn more about how to pace their play and heighten her experience? He reached for the pillow he had practiced on many times before, placed it on the bed in front of him, and lashed the crap out of it.

But each strike only fueled his anger. She told him she and Charles never—*strike*—played together—*strike*—but was that really true? *Strike*. Had she seen him play with other people? *Strike*. What did she and Charles share that they were keeping from Becca, and from him? *Strike*. Protecting Charles and his identity apparently was more important to Quinn than being open with him.

All those times she gave him short answers when he asked how it went at the club, how she shrugged off his jokes about what members did there. And the worst part was how she continued to defend Charles. How she told Jonathan not to be so self-righteous.

He raised his arm higher. *Strike! Strike! Strike!*

The fabric tore. Downy feathers sprung from the slash and wafted to the mattress, the floor, the top of his foot. He eyed the pillow tear. That's exactly how he felt—beat up, ripped apart.

And stupid. So very, very stupid.

He set the cane on the bed, wiped the sweat from his face with the towel that had started to fall loose from his waist, and hurried out of that room.

———

AFTER POURING a strong cup of coffee, he went back to his laptop and logged into email to find that message from Charles, the one with the deal memo attached. Instead of "Keep your hush money, you lying sack of shit," he typed, "Deal's off."

Pleased with his restraint, he clicked "send."

Next, the gloves were coming off, and he made a list of competing investment firms, Demeleo's rivals. When his head was clear tomorrow, he would investigate their portfolio holdings to get a feel for their investment strategies. Charles's firm might be the oldest and most influential game in town, but it wasn't the only one.

Right now, though, he opened his contacts and found the number for his old producer, Bryan, who had left the Explore Network to develop content for a boutique production company. It couldn't hurt to see what he was up to in L.A.

Heck, Jonathan could bootstrap a couple of episodes of a new show out there with the money he had. Go the DIY route and screw finding investors altogether. It would mean assuming more financial risk and it would take a lot longer, but it would also mean keeping more of the eventual profit. And having more control. There was a lot of talent and creativity in California; why couldn't he tap some of it for his own production company?

He could start slow and steady, one episode, then one series, at a time. That's how he had started his little tour business back in the day—one trip, one paying traveler other than himself at a time.

Bryan answered fast. "J.J.! You reading minds? I've been going back and forth about whether to call you. You psychic or something?"

Psychic abilities. Now those would have come in handy.

"Or something. What's up?"

"I need a location scouted and an assistant director to get three pilot episodes off the ground for a client. It's way below your pay grade J.J. and I didn't want to bother you, but I thought of you and . . . I dunno, I figured you might know someone."

"I might. What is it?"

"Reality-show type thing with a few C-listers in beach-front vacation rentals. Pretty low budget. There would be a lot of Cali travel on the front end and then they'd be on location, wherever those places end up being. The cast is good; they won't bust balls, and I have a streamer lined up to buy it."

"When's it start?" Driving the coast and playing AD did

not sound bad at all. "My pay grade's pretty low these days."

"Like, yesterday." Bryan paused. "Wait. You serious, man? What's going on? I mean, you're already a legend, having left Explore but . . . what's really up?"

"Short story, I'm in between projects and I could use a change of scenery. The rest, I'll tell you in person over a beer. Or three." He glanced at the corner of the laptop monitor. It was after eleven in New York, so the workday was about to end in L.A. He could sleep on it, call Bryan back in the morning to give him a definite answer. But what exactly was he waiting for? "Let's do it."

"Awesome, dude! That's great news. Hey. Katie and I just bought a house. It has one of those separate guest bungalow things we've been painting and re-flooring in our spare time so we can rent it out. You're welcome to stay there. Be like old times. Sorta."

Sorta meaning last time they worked together, Jonathan was running the show and Bryan worked for him.

"I need a few days to get things in order here," he said, "but let's grab that beer on the beach this weekend."

13

GONE

When Quinn pulled up to the airport terminal Thursday evening, Octavia was waiting outside. Her height and head of curls were striking among the other travelers also scanning the flow of vehicles for friends and lovers, buses and taxis and rideshares.

She had texted a couple of days ago to say Madame was actually doing better and she was flying home today, that she had reserved a car service and would catch up with Quinn Friday morning at the club.

But Quinn had texted right back and insisted on picking her up.

As they left the airport and got onto the parkway, Quinn glanced over. "So? You said she was responding to the new treatment?"

"She is. It was remarkable," Octavia said, "no one is expecting a miracle, but she's at a point where I breathed a small sigh of relief and figured I'd come home for a few weeks and then go back to see her again." She chuckled and touched Quinn's arm. "But don't worry—I have a friend who's a partner in a club in California. She already said she can fly out and cover."

"I wasn't worried," Quinn said. "If you need help when you go back, I'm here." It didn't much matter now, did it? "That's wonderful news about the treatment."

"Thank you—you're a loyal friend. Tell me, how did it go?"

"Smoothly, all things considered. No major hiccups at the club. Just one . . . kind of, I guess, personal issue."

Octavia's brown eyes were on her. "Oh? What happened?"

Quinn told her all about it as they crawled through traffic from Queens into Manhattan. How she discovered who Maximillian was at the wedding reception, how at first she assumed Becca knew he was a member but then realized she didn't. How Quinn foolishly thought she might be able to convince Charles to tell Becca so everything would be out in the open. How Jonathan saw her with Charles outside the club and assumed she was cheating. How even though she explained, he still felt betrayed. How she couldn't blame him, really, but also didn't know what else she could, or should, have done.

Octavia dropped her head and sighed. "I'm so sorry," she said as she looked up again, turning her gaze out the passenger window. "New York is one very large small town." She turned back toward Quinn. "How long has it been since you spoke to Jonathan?"

"This happened Monday. He was so angry, he wasn't hearing anything I said. And I got angry, too." She rubbed the bridge of her nose at the memory. "I told him he was just trying to use their situation to redeem himself, to make up for his ruined marriage . . ."

Octavia made a ball shape with her hands, looked at it,

and spoke in an airy voice. "I see a future in diplomacy." Quinn laughed at the fake crystal ball, the dark humor.

"Right? Not my best moment. I tried to call him that night, and since, but it always goes to voicemail. So we haven't been in touch. I know him and, unfortunately, I think that was it for us."

"It's too soon to say that." Octavia blew out another long breath. "I've had situations like this crop up in the past. It doesn't change anything, but as a member of the club you did the right thing. It's what I would have done myself, not said anything to my partner. So thank you for taking care of the place like I would. I was sure you would, that's why I asked you."

Quinn just nodded. There wasn't anything to add. She appreciated what Octavia was telling her, but no, it didn't change anything.

They were quiet, both looking out the windshield, the slow-rolling procession of red taillights in the darkness.

Octavia's phone chimed, and once she swiped open the message, she gasped. Quinn turned partially toward her, trying to keep an eye on the road.

Instantly, tears pooled at the bottom of Octavia's eyes, reflecting the highway lighting. "She's gone."

"Who's gone?"

Octavia's voice was barely a whisper. "Madame. A stroke. Chloé said it happened a little while ago." She scrolled upward, reading. "The doctor told her it would have been over fast."

"I'm so sorry." Quinn reached out and touched her forearm while looking up at the green signs over the roadway for the nearest exit. She got off and pulled onto the shoulder, put the car in park, and turned to face her friend.

Octavia blotted the corner of her eye with her finger. "It

shouldn't come as a surprise—she had been so sick. But, then she improved and . . . it's just . . . I thought . . ."

"You thought there was more time."

Octavia nodded her agreement and repeated her words. "I thought there was more time."

Quinn squeezed her arm. "I understand. I understand what it's like when you don't have as long as you expected."

"This must be so hard for you, listening to me. I'm sorry. After what you went through, I'm being selfish. I got to visit with her the last three weeks."

"It's okay. I struggled with this for a long time—I still do sometimes. Madame was aware you were there; the two of you spent important time together. So although you might not have said the actual words at the end, your relationship was so much more than that one moment. Your trip, your last weeks together, you did get to say goodbye. A meaningful goodbye."

Octavia turned toward the side window again.

"Sometime, when you're ready to talk about it, I'd love to learn more about her," Quinn added. "And about the two of you." She thought of Jonathan and how it had meant so much when he told her he wanted to hear more about her relationship with Harris. "In the meantime, why don't you stay at the farmhouse with me tonight? Company might be good."

QUINN GAVE the pillow a good shake after making up the bed in the spare room, while Octavia unpacked a few things by the dresser. "Can I make you a sandwich or some toast? Eggs? A cup of tea?" Quinn asked.

"Tea would be wonderful, and how about a scrambled

egg?" She brought her hand to her stomach. Quinn knew that sickening, unsettled sensation without her having to explain.

Octavia came over, sat on the edge of the bed, and crossed one foot over the other knee to unzip her boot. She took it off and set it on the floor, then switched legs. Although this time instead of unzipping the boot, she dropped her head in her hands.

Quinn recognized this feeling too: despair. She sat on the floor at Octavia's feet. "Let me," she said, sliding the zipper down, taking off the boot, putting it on the floor next to its mate.

Grief. It was heavy, cold. Before Harris died, Quinn had thought grief was an emotional state. Now she under- stood it was overwhelmingly physical too. It could knock you back, hold you down, press the air right out of your chest.

She rubbed Octavia's leg by the side of her knee. Quinn had planned to ask if she would go back to Paris for the funeral, if Quinn could help book a flight or cover at the club a little longer, but a teardrop landed on her hand. Now clearly wasn't the time to talk logistics.

"How about a bath while I make your food?"

Octavia nodded.

Down the hall in the guest bathroom, she opened the tub's hot water tap and placed the stopper in the drain.

It had only been a few weeks ago that Jonathan had helped her move. Not only had he drawn her a bath but also helped her undress and dry off, averting his eyes, taking care of her in such a tender way. That night had been a turning point for them, the close of one chapter and a stumbling, bittersweet opening of another.

The roar of the hot water filling the tub was not enough

to drown out the thoughts of him. Standing at the sink, she pressed her palms flat against the countertop on either side. "Damn it," she muttered, careful not to look up at the mirror.

Maybe what he said was true. Maybe he really didn't know her at all. Maybe if she looked up and into the glass, she wouldn't recognize herself either.

When the tub was full, she turned off the water and went to get Octavia. But when she approached the doorway, Octavia was exactly as Quinn had left her.

Quinn knelt in front of her again and whispered. "Bath's ready."

She let Quinn help her up and followed her down the hall. "Madame liked you. She said you reminded her of me, back when . . ." Her voice trailed off, receding like the tide.

"I liked her too. Although . . ." Quinn rubbed her bottom exaggeratedly so Octavia would see it. "She seemed to have quite the devilish side." Octavia giggled at that.

While she was in the bath, Quinn scrambled eggs and pulled a box of herbal tea out of the cabinet.

Octavia came down a little while later, wrapped in the pink robe and fuzzy slippers Quinn had left for her. Stark contrast to her usual attire. She sat at the island. "Thank you. For everything."

"I was happy to help, so it was my pleasure, all of it. Well, not the part where my life fell apart, but all the rest."

That got Octavia to laugh. "I'm really sorry it happened so soon and with someone you had multiple, close connections to—it's bad enough when you run into an acquaintance."

Quinn just listened as she poured steaming water into the mug and Octavia continued. "You know, what happened to you, with Maximillian? It's happened to me several times. I've learned to keep my circle small, and I don't socialize a lot—precisely to avoid those complications. Because once you know, you can't pretend you don't. And those relationships—as you're experiencing—inevitably change."

Quinn felt sorry for her. She did so much for others at the club so they could be themselves, but she couldn't be, at least not in New York. She was Octavia, the dominatrix, the face of the club, a persona. Suddenly, Quinn felt touched, happy to be here with this version of her. The real version that was the woman grieving the loss of a good friend, perhaps a former lover, sitting in Quinn's kitchen in a robe and slippers.

Octavia's single, strongest connection, Quinn realized, was—had been—to Madame, to a separate life she led when she went to Paris. But going to France two or three times a year was not a whole lot of connection to sustain you. Octavia's reserve, her independence, her devotion to the club and lifestyle—before tonight, Quinn had only seen her let her guard down that weekend at the château in France, and now it made sense.

"It sounds solitary," Quinn said.

Octavia paused for a second, then shrugged. "It might be. But it suits me, and it's what I chose."

She finished the eggs and tea and padded upstairs to bed, while Quinn washed the dishes and set them in the drainer to dry.

The next morning, as Quinn tiptoed down the hall toward the stairs, she was surprised to see the spare bedroom door open and Octavia awake, dressed, and sitting on the edge of the bed. She was staring into space, forlorn.

"Hey. Good morning. How are you doing?" Quinn asked.

Octavia pressed her hand to her chest, indicating that's where she felt it, and squeezed her lips, trying to hold back tears. Quinn sat next to her and took hold of her other hand. "I know." *I know how it feels.* "What can I do?"

But although she knew the depth and hold of grief, she hated being so powerless to ease Octavia's pain. "Come here," she whispered, putting an arm around Octavia's shoulder. Octavia leaned against her, and Quinn rubbed her back as she wept.

Octavia and Manon had a unique and unconventional relationship—Quinn could tell that much—and trying to piece together their history made her long for Jonathan. Theirs, too, was unique and unconventional. In their earliest hours together, they had gone places Quinn couldn't have imagined, each of them, for different reasons, proving to be unknown but captivating territory to the other.

During one of their early nights together, the night he laid behind her after sex and held her, she had wanted to move away. But even as distraught and isolated as she was, in her new reality his arms felt right. That feeling had only intensified. Before Jonathan, she had given up imagining the future, and now she couldn't envision it without him.

Octavia's phone chirped on the nightstand. As she read, she smiled sadly, then held out the phone to show Quinn the message. "It's from Chloé."

> Bonjour. I hope I am not waking you. It is hard not to mourn the void in our lives today, but we both know she did not want that. She asked me, when the time came, to deliver this message to you immediately, with a letter she left with me for you to follow when we next see each other:

"There will be no dreary funeral, darling, only a party. A magical party. You must come. Bring Quinn. A party in Paris will do you both good. Chloé will work with you to find a suitable date. No tears, mon bijou — I can't bear to think of you sad."

A single tear descended from the corner of her eye, and she wiped it away, attempting to obey the spirit of Manon's wishes. "Would you come with me?"

"Yes, of course. I think so. I mean . . . Listen to me stumbling. I would love to, but if Jonathan and I, if there's any hope of salvaging this, I'd like to talk to him first, include him in the decision-making."

All along, he hadn't felt like he was a full part of her life; for much of their time together, she hadn't let him. But that had changed. And although he might be convinced their relationship was over, she would not yet let go—not without telling him how she really felt.

The timing had been awful. Once she was ready to say it, to tell him she loved him, Charles's secret had snuck between them.

Octavia seemed to read her thought. "He could come with us."

"We are a very long way from having that particular conversation."

This time Octavia put her arm around Quinn's shoulder and affectionately jostled her. "It's going to be okay. We're both going to be okay."

Quinn leaned against her. "I know, but I can't stand not talking to him." She had tended to Octavia since picking her up last night, but her own feelings, the ache in her chest, had not been far from her awareness. "At least to explain things again when we're both calmer and to tell him in no uncertain terms how I feel about him."

Deep regret had been one of the hardest things to face when Harris died. There wasn't much you could do with regret, except channel it into motivation to handle a similar situation differently in the future. A sense of urgency gripped her, spurred her to take a gulp of breath and stand up. "I need to go to him—I'm sorry to up and leave, but . . ."

"Don't be sorry." Octavia stood and put a few items of clothing into her bag. "I'll go with you—I need to get to the club. When's the next train?"

14

SURPRISE

Within forty-eight hours of talking to Bryan, Jonathan had his place sublet—to an actress doing a Broadway show who wanted to live closer to the theater. By Friday morning, he had packed the things he was taking to California into a carry-on roller bag, his old backpack, and his laptop bag. The fridge was empty, and he had written out a page of instructions and emergency maintenance phone numbers for the renter.

The spare bedroom was back to its former self. He had covered the dungeon furniture with sheets and hauled it to his locked storage room in the basement—at five a.m. so no one would see him. He had checked in for the flight, scored a window seat in first class—a free upgrade thanks to all his unused miles—and hired Gil to pick him up in a couple of hours.

Good to go.

The L.A. gig wasn't exactly a step up career-wise, but he needed to regroup, and California wasn't a bad place to do that. He could wear T-shirts every day, work on the tan he never got, practice being mellow, and pretend he always wanted to learn to surf. Maybe he would even take a couple lessons on the weekends.

Other key selling points included the fact that he could help out his buddy and a young director with their show. And he would be busy, which he would embrace and not think about Quinn. Or Charles. Or how his insides felt under the influence of so many shitty feelings when he thought about them.

He looked at his phone screen again. It was early, granted, but. . . Nothing. After those few calls from her that he had ignored, she hadn't bothered to try again. *Guilty conscience.*

He put clean sheets on the bed and, with nothing left to do, took the elevator down and went for a brisk walk, stuffing his hands in his pockets to keep them warm.

The fall's first morning frost glittered on the leaves in the tree beds along the sidewalk, and the wind blew away his exhaled breath. Yes, California sun would be an improvement.

He walked a strangely shaped route, careful to avoid the street where Octavia's was, the street of Charles's company headquarters, and any streets where he had been with Quinn. Together the constraints ate up a surprising, depressing, amount of Manhattan real estate.

California would be great for that too. He could go where he wanted, no ghostly reminders of the past haunting him at every turn.

When he got back to his building, Gil was waiting, twenty minutes early and leaning against his black sedan, smoking. "I'll run up and get my stuff—be back in a minute," Jonathan said after they shook hands and Gil commented about the changing weather.

Gil put out his cigarette in a portable ashtray and

pushed off the car to follow Jonathan. "Let me give you a hand."

"That's okay—I got it," Jonathan told him. He was paying Gil to give him a ride, not kiss his ass. "It's just a coupla bags."

The elevator zipped him up to the landing. Before grabbing the bags, he went to the living room windows and gazed out. Going to California was the right thing to do. His terrace with the nice year-round furniture and the romantic lighting and incredible view of the city—he loved it here. But as great as it was, now it all just reminded him of Quinn. Of the nights they spent out here, the conversations, the explorations. And now, the betrayal.

Okay, enough of that.

He double-checked that the sliding glass doors were locked and put his stuff in the elevator.

He swiped his key card, which he needed to remember to give to Barnes on his way out for the renter. The numbered lights blinked as the elevator descended floor by floor.

AS SHE APPROACHED his building's entrance, she recognized his driver, Gil, leaning against the black car parked at the curb. It was the same man she had somehow mustered the courage to send away that first night with Jonathan. Her cheeks heated at the recollection.

He smiled and stepped toward her, loafers polished to a shine, hand extended. "Good morning," he said, upbeat and friendly.

"Morning." She tried to return his level of joviality as

she looked into the dark windows. "Is Jonathan—" she pointed toward the car.

"Just getting his luggage," Gil said, gesturing upward toward the building. "He should be down in a minute. You know, we could have picked you up—you didn't have to take the train in."

"Luggage?" she asked, before it hit her that Gil assumed she would be traveling with Jonathan.

He pointed between her and the car, puzzled. "Aren't you . . . going also?"

She shook her head no. "I'm afraid not."

His phone pinged faintly, and he took it out of his breast pocket. "He's on his way down."

She hadn't planned on Jonathan traveling, and she was not going to talk to him standing out here on the street.

"I'd love to surprise him," she said to Gil as she opened the front passenger door. "Before you close his door, I'll hop out and jump in the back after him."

He gave her a conspiratorial smile, followed by the slightest hint of suspicion but thankfully not enough to say no. "Of course, as you wish."

She got in and shimmied down so her head was below the window. In the rearview mirror, she could see Jonathan's frame fill the building entrance as he stopped to speak to Barnes. They both laughed, although Jonathan's face looked strained, his eyes sad. She could see that from here because she knew that face, those eyes. The two men shook hands, and now he was headed toward the car.

Gil opened the rear door, and Jonathan got in and slid toward the center of the bench. The two of them discussed the best route as Jonathan checked traffic on his phone. Gil took a step back to give her space to maneuver.

Staying low and quiet, she slid out of the car and

hurried around the open door, behind Gil, and into the back beside Jonathan.

"What the—?" Gil shut the door, closing them in, and a moment later the car inched away from the curb. With a honk at a pushy cab, he slipped into the slow flow of the morning rush.

At least the conversation wouldn't be hurried, and a sense of hope stirred in her chest. A divider rose between the front and the back, Gil giving them privacy. He probably thought they were going to . . . Well, what they *might* have done alone in the backseat if things were different.

"What. Are. You. Doing?" His voice sounded cold. Rocky and desolate.

She angled her body to face him. It was so good to see him, although he looked tired, bereft. Like she felt. "I know you're angry, and I was trying to give you some time but—"

"So thoughtful," he interrupted.

On the train into the city earlier, she had thought about what she wanted to say but not word for word, and she hadn't counted on such a stiff, discouraging expression. That was not helping her thought-gathering process, so she just launched into it.

"Jonathan, I can't force you to understand why I didn't tell you. And I can't make you believe Charles and I weren't having an affair, or playing together at the club—we weren't, but I know keeping *any*thing from you was the very worst way I could have hurt you. I'm truly, truly sorry."

He wouldn't look at her. "Can you hear how meaningless that apology sounds?" He spoke to the closed window, staring outward. "I mean, do you actually hear yourself? Keeping *something* from me, and from Becca? Whatever you choose to call your relationship with him, that's a big something." The rasp in his voice reminded her of a gravel road, of jagged, cold stones.

She had expected him still to be angry, but already she had underestimated it.

"It was a big omission, you're right," she said, lowering her gaze and pushing the cuticle on her index fingernail down with the opposite thumbnail. "But I could not tell you. And what would you have done if I had? Confronted Charles? Confronted Becca? What would have given you the right to betray confidences and insert yourself into their business, their relationship, like that?"

"Why don't you tell me, Quinn, since you seem to have a real knack for betraying confidences and involving yourself in others' relationships?" He cleared his throat. "Did you miss the memo, the one where I told you I was in love with you?" His voice cracked when he said *love*. "In protecting theirs, you ruined ours."

Now she was the one who needed to look away. The ice in his eyes was too much. It gouged a piece of her heart like the sharp edge of a glacier.

They were quiet as Gil headed into the Midtown Tunnel.

After a while, she broke their silence. "Where are you going?"

"L.A."

"What are you doing there?"

"Producing a show for a friend," he answered without looking at her.

"How long will you be gone?"

He dropped his head and shook it from side to side. "Let's not do this—the chit-chat crap."

They were quiet again, each facing their own window

onto an entirely different view, the roiling tension between them about to bubble over.

"Damn it, Quinn. Why did you do this?" he finally asked, gesturing at the cabin surrounding them.

"I needed to see you. I needed to tell you again how sorry I am." She knew how the next thing she was about to say would sound, how forced and awkward and discordant, but if she had gotten to his building two minutes later he would already be gone and who knew when, or if, she would have another opportunity.

She had to say it.

"I realize you might never understand or forgive me, but I still want you to know—I love you. I've wanted to tell you, but not with this thing between us. That was another reason I was trying to get Charles to tell her, so it would be out in the open, no secrets between you and me." She reached across the seat for his hand, but his huff of a laugh stopped her cold. Her eyes welled immediately, as if they received the message before her ears heard the sound.

The car slowed. They had arrived at La Guardia. Gil pulled over and, just like that, Jonathan pulled the door handle and stepped out in front of the terminal.

He said a few words to Gil and the trunk slammed, shaking the interior. As she opened her door to get out to say goodbye, he hurried toward the airport's glass doors and disappeared inside.

She looked up, caught sight of him on the escalator in his faded brown leather jacket. He was in the terminal's glass tower, some new, expensive architectural feature the city had made a huge fuss about, something to do with enabling travelers to say one more goodbye before embarking on their journey. Under different circumstances, she would have appreciated the symbolism, the metaphor.

She kept her eye on him as long as she could. Two levels up, there was the caramel-colored jacket again, standing by the glass. Was he able to see her?

He put his open palm against the window, then made a fist and banged the heel of his hand, slowly, shaking his head as if reminding himself, *no*.

HE HAD SETTLED into his seat in the front cabin, nearly two flutes of champagne in before the captain announced a fifteen-plus aircraft queue for takeoff. He didn't drink much when he flew; it only made the jet lag worse. Today, however, he was making an exception.

Outside the window, airport workers scurried around stationary planes. They dragged hoses and de-iced wings and loaded luggage onto conveyor belts, while marshallers waved orange batons to guide the birds to the runway.

What the hell just happened?

He had been stunned by Quinn's balls the night of the dinner party, when she sent Gil packing, but he was utterly, entirely flabbergasted now. How could she ambush him like that, sneaking into the car and, Jesus H., telling him she *loved* him? As he was about to get on a plane and leave town? Did she think that would make it all okay, saying the words, although they came with a big fucking lie behind them?

She made her choice. Jonathan wasn't it. Her relationship with Becca, after throwing the poor woman's wedding reception, wasn't it. Her new quote *lifestyle*—that was it, that's what she picked. That's why it struck him as funny, so pathetically funny, when she said she loved him.

A week ago, he would have given up a nut to hear her

say it. He downed the last swig of champagne from the flute. He couldn't shake the image of her eyes filling with tears when he laughed, pulled his hand away from hers, got the hell out of the car. He couldn't look at her again after he saw those eyes or, even as pissed off as he was, he wouldn't have been able to board this flight.

If he had kept his gaze on her, against his better judgment, he would have let her take his hand. He would have pulled her into him and held her, kissed the top of her head while he whispered that they would figure it out together, work it out somehow, that it would all be okay.

But it would not be okay, not this time.

The flight attendant standing by the galley walked down the aisle toward him, paused by his seat, and touched his shoulder. "May I take your glass?"

He handed it over. "Could I get a refill, please?" She held his eyes, probably trying to assess how he would hold his liquor for the next five hours, and probably thinking, *Pace yourself, tiger*.

"Certainly. Be right back." The touch on his shoulder again. The way she didn't use "sir" with him, the way she swung the flute upwards as she took it from him, the way she walked away with a bit more swing in her hips than on her way down the aisle a few moments ago—he wondered if she was flirting, if maybe she recognized him.

People were funny when it came to that, confusing familiarity from seeing his mug on television with thinking they knew him.

Just as she reached the galley, the captain announced they were up soon for takeoff and flight attendants should take a seat.

She nodded at him—*don't worry; I got this*—and disappeared behind the divider, then re-emerged a few seconds later holding a full flute.

She walked quickly and handed him the glass low, as if to shield it from others' view.

"Here you go, 8-A. This should hold you through take-off. Don't let it fly out of your hands, or I'll get in trouble." She smiled as if they shared a secret.

Bells and chimes sounded, and she walked to the front of the cabin, then again disappeared behind the partition as another flight attendant made announcements. He could picture her lowering the jump seat, slipping her arms through the vertical straps of the belt.

The plane sped over the runway, and soon the wheels left the tarmac. The aircraft rose higher and higher, bumped through the thick clouds, and leveled off in an intense azure sky. Another set of chimes rang and the seatbelt light darkened. He counted rows as the flight attendant returned. Three, four, five, six, seven, and here she was.

Actually, she passed him and drew the curtain behind his seat to divide the cabins. Her hand grazed his shoulder again, less accidental this time, more familiar. "Doin' okay 8-A? I'll take your glass if you're finished."

"Doin' fine. Thank you."

When she came by again later, she was wearing an apron, pushing the drinks cart.

"What'll it be, 8-A? Gin and tonic? Bloody Mary? Whiskey neat? Am I warm?"

"Very. Surprise me."

She mixed a Bloody Mary, added a piece of celery—ah, the perks of first class—and set the glass down with a napkin on his tray. Then she added a can of mix and a mini bottle of vodka beside it. "In case you get thirsty—or lonely," she said, smiling.

When the next cart came by with food, he declined and, once it passed, pulled a crushed sandwich out of the outer pocket of his laptop bag. Airline food was often loaded with salt, which contributed to dehydration, which, on top of drinking too much booze, worsened jet lag. He had done research on this for his show, since he and his crew—make that former crew—dealt with it all the time and had tried just about every remedy under the sun.

When he had his tour company, he would schedule the first day lightly so people could acclimate, but his TV crew had to hit the ground running. The blog posts he had written on jet lag were among the most popular on the show's website and his social media feeds. Except for the ones on others' blogs and feeds about his affair.

A different flight attendant cleared plates, silverware, and glasses. He handed over his crumpled plastic sandwich foil but kept his glass, set it in the cupholder, and tucked the spare bottle of vodka between his thigh and the seat divider. A steward came by with coffee and tea. "No, thanks," he said. When the cleanup was done, the cabin lights dimmed.

He reclined his seat, closed the shade to block the cheerful sun, and wondered how he was going to fill the next four hours with some activity other than replaying his car ride with Quinn, the montage of key moments in their relationship that his mind had glommed onto the past few days, and the images of her with Charles outside the club. The way she had touched him, comforted him, Jonathan felt as if he had witnessed a private moment, as if *he* were the interloper. One more bottle of vodka wasn't going to take care of any of that.

And then the flight attendant was back, without the apron. "Still doin' okay, 8-A?" Her voice was lower now, more like a husky whisper.

"Still doin' okay."

"It's Jonathan, right? Jonathan Jaines? From *Spice of Life*?"

"That would be me." He put his finger to his lips. "Don't want chaos breaking out. All the adoring fans."

She laughed, the long curls that had been swept into a bun and held with a pen during drink service now bounced down her back in a ponytail.

"It'll be our little secret. I'll keep calling you 8-A, and I won't ask you to autograph a cocktail napkin. I'd prefer to keep you to myself."

He coughed. Spit had gone down the wrong tube.

"Careful, 8-A." She put her hand on his shoulder again, then patted his upper back and lowered her voice while she kept rubbing. "It must not be easy to go anywhere, with so many people wanting a piece of you."

He fought the reflex to cough again. "First world problem. I'd never complain about that." Only after he said it did he realize his agreement might have accidentally opened a door he hadn't meant to crack.

"Well, good then," she said. "I have a mandated break in ten minutes, and I'll be in the private crew cabin—the door is behind row forty. There's a flight of stairs just inside." She had stopped rubbing his back and now she smoothed his shirt at the shoulder. "If I can do anything to make your flight more . . . enjoyable . . . don't hesitate to come find me."

15

A FEW WORDS

S tanding at the counter, she looked out the kitchen window above the sink. Raindrops slid down the glass, a cold, dreary autumn shower.

Jonathan had not been in touch since he left last week. Not that she expected to hear from him after how he practically tripped over his own feet to leap out of the car. And especially after how he laughed. The hurt, the shame at how her declaration sounded because her timing had been so wrong, still pricked at her heart when she thought about it.

Even so, she checked her phone. In case.

Nothing.

Of course, nothing. She had been looking at it more than was sane. Each time she turned it over, hope fluttered. Maybe this time she would have a text from him waiting. A text like, *I'm sorry for how I reacted.*

Or, *I've been waiting to hear you say those words—I love you, too.*

Or, *Why don't you come out to California and join me? This trip was a mistake. I miss you.*

Yes, any of these would be good. But a gnome in a polka dot hat landing on her doorstop would be more likely. Or a fairy with leopard spots. And three wings. With such fantastical thinking, she should consider writing children's books.

She put the phone back on the counter, screen down. From here forward, she would not check it unless it made a noise that warranted a look—a ding, a chime, a vibration. She needed to institute rules, face the facts.

Jonathan wasn't going to call or text.

She couldn't avoid Becca forever.

And, Quinn had not changed her mind about not outing Charles.

Until he told Becca, Quinn remained a reluctant but complicit keeper of his secret.

If she were writing this situation in one of her books, this would be the point in the story where her character would have an epiphany that suddenly and likely dramatically crystallized the change she needed to make. She would know what she needed to do, toughen up, and do it.

Dig deep, act brave.

But she was sorely lacking an epiphany.

And unlike the third-act decisions in her novels, the choice at the crux of her dilemma, her choice not to tell Becca about Charles, would not change. She was a member of Octavia's, part of the lifestyle, however vanilla or clothed or infrequently she chose to practice it. And it was part of her.

She kept thinking about how she and Jonathan could be together, what their resolution might be. She wanted one so much. But it wasn't coming. Maybe that was the epiphany, that there was no good solution. Maybe it was more this quiet knowing and acceptance despite the costs, rather than discovery.

But that didn't mean it wasn't breaking her heart—or that she couldn't still fight for the man she loved. Only how do you fight for someone and also tell them, if I had to do it over I would make the same choice. I might have to hurt you like that again.

It was heartbreaking to admit because she knew what it meant for them.

It amounted to trust, pure and simple, didn't it? He had told her he trusted her before—trusted her to manage the club, trusted that her interactions there wouldn't cross any line.

It wasn't enough.

He trusted her in the situations he could conceive of, but neither of them had imagined the scenario with Charles.

If they were to have a future together, he would have to trust her unconditionally. Other things might occur at the club that she couldn't share with him, and he would have to trust her actions, her decisions, her principles. Her love.

They had fallen far; he wasn't likely to reach that degree of trust any time soon. If at all. If they were to have a future together, it would require forgiveness on his part and some open line of communication.

Would they ever find their way back to what they had started to build?

Start small. Just write a few words. That's what Harris used to say to her when she would sit down to write but struggled with how to begin a new book, a new chapter, a new scene. Often it was the only prompt she needed to get going again—his confident voice, his belief in her, his encouragement.

She reached for her phone and turned it over. This time, she didn't expectantly look for a message. Instead, she opened a fresh one, a miniature blank digital page. She tapped the keys just as the thoughts came to her, no self-criticism, no editing.

A small start, a few words.

> Hi. I don't expect you to answer. Just wondering, how it's going out there?

She paused, watched out the window for a few seconds as heavy raindrops spattered the river, and looked back at her screen.

> It's raining here. I hope you have some sun.

QUINN DIALED Becca's number and, before she even heard it ring, Becca answered with an upbeat "Heyyy." Knowing Becca, she had the phone at her side, bored already with bedrest.

"How are you?" Quinn asked.

"Good. Relieved . . . happy. The doctor called it a false alarm, but I'm still not supposed to do much. Or, anything. I'm going a little crazy, honestly."

Quinn heard rustling in the background, and Becca whispered. "No, I don't need anything, I'm fine. Sorry, I'm back," she said louder again. "Charles is going out for some groceries." Her voice lowered once more. "Thank goodness. I get to be by myself for a half-hour. He's so worried, he won't leave me alone for a second."

It was pretty clear Charles hadn't talked to her yet. "He had quite a scare—we all did. But I'm so happy you're feeling good. Being bored and catered to for a few weeks doesn't sound too terrible."

"I know. And I can work from home and read a lot of new mom and baby stuff. It's all good—we're really lucky."

"I would say so. You're going to be a wonderful mom, honey. I'm so excited for you. For you both."

She forced the image out of her mind of Charles in his mask.

"You're the best, always in my corner. Hey, how are *you* doing? My mom mentioned Jonathan's on the West Coast? Charles said it must have been some project he committed to before they decided to do their new company thing together."

"Yes, he's in L.A." She swallowed the lump forming in her throat.

"How long will he be gone?"

"You know, I'm not exactly sure."

"It's great he could slip this in. You didn't want to go with him? You two lovebirds haven't been apart much lately."

Quinn forced a laugh and took a breath to steady herself. This is why she had put off calling Becca to check in—there were too many things she could not say. "It's more of a business trip, and this way he can focus and finish more quickly."

That wasn't a lie—she did want him to finish quickly and come back to New York. Three-thousand miles would not help heal the rift between them.

Becca sighed. "I wish we could catch up over dinner or tea. If you want to come over, I'm here, like, *alllways*. And maybe Charles will actually leave the apartment for more than an hour if he knows you'll babysit me."

She wanted to say yes and visit. But Becca and her husband had unfinished business.

Quinn needed to step back. "I'd love to see you, honey. Right now, though, you need to rest, and I have some things to get sorted." *And so do you, you just might not know it yet.* "But we'll find a time soon. In the meantime, I'm thinking about you."

They ended the call and she set her phone on the counter again. Where it would stay—here in the kitchen. It didn't need to be in her hand twenty-four-seven.

She went up to her bedroom to get a sweater from the closet. The house was warm, but the weather, her heart—a chill was setting in. As she closed the closet door, the drawing of Jonathan in Paris caught her eye from its corner of her bureau mirror.

What had he done with her drawing when he left New York? Tucked it in the side pocket of his bag to bring along, torn it up, forgotten it entirely? She looked at it closely. He thought he had seen her in the shop, and his expression showed surprise, good surprise. Something like hopefulness.

Although they hadn't known it, their paths had crossed in Paris. Not just the same city on the same weekend, but the same street, the same shop, the same moment on a blindingly sunny Sunday morning.

She thought of Octavia and Madame Manon, of Jonathan relishing his role as dominant while Quinn managed the club, of his leaving the network and striking out on his own, of her discovery of Maximillian's identity at the wedding.

Truth really could be stranger than fiction. She could not have made this story up if she tried.

This story.

Their story.

The feeling that overcame her just then was an old, familiar one. Her pulse picked up. A whorl of excited energy uncoiled in her chest, expanding to a shiver and then to tingling along the side of her hand, as if it were brushing across a notebook page as she wrote. The books she was most proud of writing, and the ones that had gone on to be the most successful, had started with sensations like these. *Exactly like these.*

She went to her office, sat at her desk, picked up one of the new notebooks she bought in Paris.

So what if Leigh didn't like a few pages of writing she had sent? That was experimental; this story was different.

Start small. Just write a few words.

She picked up her old pen, pressing some circles into the paper to get the ink to flow.

And then she wrote.

Just a few words.

And then a few words more.

She wrote until her hand cramped and her stomach growled and her shoulder began to ache.

The sun set over the river, a thin fiery line amid the clouds.

The white-lined notebook pages stiffened from the imprint of so many words from the pen's ball point, and they crackled as she fanned through them.

It was late. She was done for now, but only just getting started.

It was easy to write this way, simply telling the story as she remembered it unfolding in her mind's eye, one moment, one event, one experience after the other.

She didn't wonder what critics or readers would say, she

just put the words on the page. Easy, because it would never see the light of day.

SHE MADE A SANDWICH, wrapped it in a paper towel, put on her gloves and scarf and coat, and headed outside. The rain had stopped. At the river's edge, she sat on the boulder. The moon shined white-gold, a hair off full, and twinkled on the lapping water.

It was three hours earlier in California. What was he doing? She tried to think about something else, and when that didn't last for five seconds, she put down the sandwich, took off her gloves, fished her phone out of her coat pocket, and typed.

> I know you won't answer. I hope you do, but I'm going to write anyway. How are you settling in? What's the project like? How's L.A.? I was only there that one time, when we filmed for Market Day. I wrote today. Really wrote. It felt so natural, like meeting someone you've been close to, who's been a part of you, after a long absence. I miss you.

Why, exactly, was she doing this to herself?

This was one question she actually knew the answer to. She was a writer. Composing was her way of being in the world. Her way of figuring out. Her way of understanding, of connecting.

She hadn't done the wrong thing. Her choice hurt him terribly, yes, but she wasn't giving up. He had said and done cutting things in anger—his laughter, saying he didn't know her. But she knew *him*, the kind, vulnerable man who worried he wouldn't measure up, the man who silently understood what Quinn needed and had put his own needs aside again and again to give it to her. Who had bared his feelings, who had finally started to take.

The one who had soothed her closed, broken heart and gave her hope. She would not, could not, give up on that man.

She put the phone back in her pocket and looked out at the water. An owl hooted in the trees nearby; a train passed in the distance; her phone vibrated against her side.

Fumbling to pull it out, she turned it right-side-up and looked at the screen.

It wasn't Jonathan, it was Charles calling. *Not a problem with Becca's pregnancy. Please, no, not that.*

"Is she okay?" Quinn blurted in place of a greeting, suddenly shivering in the night air.

There was silence for a second or two and when he finally spoke, his voice was different—heavy, sad. She squeezed her eyes and clenched her fist. *Please let her be alright.*

"I'm not sure how to answer that. She knows my . . . secret . . . now—the lifestyle, the club, all of it. We did not talk about anyone else. What you choose to share or not share about your own life is up to you. As I have said all along."

"Okay. Okay. Well, that's good. I mean good that it's not the preg . . ." She stopped herself from stumbling further. Nothing about this, except the fact that he wasn't calling about Becca's health, was good. "Thank you for telling me."

Again, silence. Because, she realized, he had already hung up.

The sense of relief she had imagined would come from this moment did not materialize.

There would be so many pieces to put back together. How long would it take to figure out how they now fit?

If they fit.

There was no going back to the way things used to be. If she learned anything these last eighteen months, it was that.

16

NOT THAT MANY DUNGEONS

The call Quinn dreaded came three days later, while she was at her desk writing. It was now Becca's voice that was heavy and sad.

"Can I talk to you?" she asked. "I didn't know who else to call. I can't talk to my mom, or my friends, about this."

"Of course, talk to me." Quinn didn't ask what was wrong because she already knew.

"The other day I was joking with Charles about something—I can't remember what I said exactly, but it was something about whips and handcuffs—and he got all serious and said he needed to talk to me. And then he told me this . . . this . . . He told me that he's into S&M, that he's been going to a club. I thought he was *joking*. I thought he was being funny, sarcastic, so I kept teasing him about it, making these crazy statements about him tying me up on a rack and handcuffing me and telling me to call him master and . . .

"At some point I noticed he was staring at the ground with his shoulders all forward, like a little boy who got caught doing something wrong. I swear, he didn't look like himself; he looked like a totally different person. That's when I realized. It wasn't a joke. He was telling me the truth. He had this whole secret life he kept from me. I feel like such an *idiot*."

"You're not an idiot."

"And the wedding. Our *wedding*. I can't believe I didn't suspect it, that I didn't notice any signs. I *married* him. You did such an incredible thing for us, and it means nothing now—it was all a lie." Her voice cracked, and she began to cry.

Quinn wished she could hug Becca and take hold of her shoulders through the phone. "It didn't mean nothing. It meant everything. To all of us, but especially to him."

"You're wrong. I asked him how long he had been into this, how long he had been *not* telling me." Quinn's gut clenched. "It went back to before we *met*. How could I not have suspected anything?"

"Because he made sure you didn't. Because he kept it from you, because he was trying to protect you. I'm sure he didn't want you to think any less of him."

She could picture Becca, her bouncy hair limp, her wide eyes rimmed red from crying. She sniffled. "I just don't understand any of this. I told him I was going to go back to my mom's until the baby . . ."

"No, honey, no," Quinn interrupted. "Don't do anything out of anger or hurt." She pictured Jonathan escaping from his car, hitting the terminal window with the heel of his hand, and how bad watching that had felt. "I know it's incredibly hard, but give it some time before you make a decision."

"That's what he said. With the pregnancy, and the stress, he begged me to stay here." She started to cry again. "He basically moved into his study. And I can hardly pee without him asking if I'm okay. He canceled all his upcoming trips—at least the ones that were actual trips and not lies—and he's been apologizing, like, constantly."

"He loves you so much."

"That's what I don't understand. How do you live a lie with someone you love? How do you *do* that?"

"He hid a part of himself from you. He must have had very compelling reasons, because he is mad about you. I could see it in his eyes, everyone could—that man worships you."

"But you don't really know him either."

Quinn inhaled and sat straighter. "Not well, no. But I might understand more about this than you realize."

Becca started to speak, but Quinn kept on. She had to or she would chicken out. "I need to tell you something, something I haven't even told your mom."

She wouldn't ask Becca not to tell Leigh. She would not ask anyone to keep a secret from someone they were close to. "Your mom doesn't know because, like Charles, I hid a part of myself from her. I didn't think she would understand, and I didn't want her to think less of me because of it —I know there's no reason to, but not everyone gets that. What I haven't told her, or you, is that I might be able to understand what Charles has done, living a double life, because I've experimented with that lifestyle too. And I've kept it quiet."

Breathe.

"Experimented with Jonathan, you mean?"

"Yes, at first with him. And then I wanted to learn more about it so I went to a club, a dungeon. Not a sex club, and I never cheated on him, not even close. It was a way for me to explore something I was curious about without the . . . complications . . . of a relationship I wasn't ready for."

Little did I guess I would meet your husband there.

"Wow, I had no idea. Thank you for sharing that." Becca paused. "See, I knew I could talk to you—I totally get why you didn't tell my mom. She can be judgy."

A chuckle escaped from Quinn's throat. "You had no idea because I didn't let you, or her, have any idea. I walled off that part of my life, that part of myself. I did it to protect myself from what the people I love might think. So I can understand how Charles might have done the same."

Because he's a wicked dom and probably afraid you would think he was some kind of monster.

"Jonathan was okay with you going to a club, a dungeon? I don't mean to pry, but do you have an open relationship?"

"We didn't." Past tense. "And we didn't need to, although that's an option for couples. For many people, sex is involved, but it doesn't have to be." She shared Octavia's analogy. "This might be a funny parallel, but a friend, someone I have a lot of respect for, shared it with me and I'm passing it on: Think of it like fast food. You don't have to order the whole combo meal; you can simply order the fries."

Becca laughed, and Quinn relaxed the tiniest bit. "There are as many options and arrangements as there are relationships. If you asked Jonathan, which you can—I'm sure he'd talk to you about what it was like for him—he'd probably say that he *wasn't* really okay with me going to the club. I think he wished that what we did within our relationship would satisfy my curiosity and that I wouldn't need anything else. But he accepted it, just like I accepted things about him I wasn't one-hundred percent comfortable with. That's the reality of relationships, the beauty of partnership —acceptance and compromise."

"Is it just me with super-sensitive pregnancy hormones, or are you deliberately speaking in the past tense about you two?"

"It's not you, sweetie. We've had some issues lately."

Quinn would not blurt out that she knew about Charles. As they had been talking, she decided to use the same strategy as her friends who had kids employed to talk about sex. Don't put all the information out there at once; let them ask the questions as they're ready and able to process. Becca was no child, obviously—she was a mature, whip-smart young woman—but this situation was a lot for anyone to absorb. Piling on more than she wanted or was ready to hear would only set them back further.

"What if you try to focus more on the future than the past?" she asked Becca. "And as you look ahead, you don't have to fully embrace it; as a couple you can find something that works for you *both*, a balance. I'm confident you can."

"But you and Jonathan weren't able to."

The story hasn't ended yet.

"We were actually able to make it work. But then things got more complicated than either of us had considered."

There was an unforeseen plot twist.

"I just don't know if I can get past all the lies he must have had to tell me."

"I understand, sweetie. I'm sure it tore him up to lie to you. But I also believe it came from a place of wanting to protect you."

"Protect me from what, exactly?"

"Only he can answer that, but I can imagine he might have wanted to protect you from himself. He might have felt ashamed—and scared. He adores you so much, he wouldn't want to risk that you wouldn't understand or that you would see him differently. Or maybe he didn't think you would want to participate, and then what? He would be forced to make a heartbreaking choice, giving up a part of himself—and being less whole, less happy, because of it—or giving you up. He couldn't bear to let you go, so, little by little, this separate part of himself took on its own life."

"You're freaking me out a little. That's exactly what he said. Almost word for word."

"Keep talking to him. Please. Talk about what he needs and what you need. You'll have to figure out how much you're willing to share with him. Maybe all of it, maybe none of it, and maybe a lot of wonderful things in between. It could be an incredibly exciting adventure for you as a couple, and once you get past this point in your marriage, I guarantee it will bring you even closer than you were before."

"It's hard to picture that, with all the lies . . . And he told me he had a, a . . . playmate. But that they never had sex."

Quinn pictured the collared woman in the harness of knots. "He's going to have to regain your trust. And you'll have to learn to trust him again. But now that this is out in the open, things will be a lot less black and white; it's not an either-or choice. You love everything else about him, don't you?"

"Yes."

"And he loves you. He has you on a pedestal a hundred feet high. Anyone can see that."

"You sound so calm and wise. I'm not there yet."

Quinn bit the inside of her lip. She was anything but calm. Becca still didn't know the full story.

"I was considering going to one—a dungeon—to see what it's about. But, with being pregnant . . ." Her voice grew softer. Quinn pictured her glancing down, cradling her belly.

"Right now might not be the best time, but that's a great idea—the two of you going together."

"Actually, I don't know if I'm ready to do that with him. But maybe I could go with *you* sometime, to the one you go to."

Here's where it got complicated, she wanted to say. She opened her mouth to speak, but Becca jumped in. "Hey, wait. There can't be *that* many dungeons around here. Did you ever bump into him?"

Quinn steadied herself before she provided the level of detail Becca finally asked for. "Yes, in fact. I didn't know who he was at the time, but yes. I realized toward the end of your wedding reception that he was someone I had seen at the club."

Becca inhaled sharply, a drawn out gasp.

"At first, I assumed you knew. But even if you didn't, it wasn't my place to tell you. For a lot of reasons."

"You knew."

"Not until that moment at the reception. I hadn't recognized him before that." *He always wore a mask.* But that detail, too, was not for Quinn to share.

"He was leading a double life, and you knew and didn't tell me. You protected him."

"I protected his privacy like I would protect anyone else from the club if I ran into them in another setting. Not so different from how I didn't tell Jonathan about you being pregnant when you asked me not to say anything."

Becca scoffed. "But you protected his privacy from *me*."

"He was the one to tell you, not me. It's between the two of you to figure out in your own way, in your own time. But I am so sorry."

"So I really am the last to find out. Wait, did Jonathan know?"

"No. I couldn't tell him either. But he knows now—although not because I told him. The day you went to the hospital, I was at the club. Charles had been there with me, so when Jonathan came by to pick me up to go to you, he saw us."

There was no sharp inhale this time, only Becca's voice, deep and slow. "Define 'with me.'"

"Charles was there because I asked him to talk face to face—to talk about how I couldn't keep this secret any longer, knowing how much covering it up would hurt you. And hurt Jonathan. And hurt your mom. Basically, everyone he and I both care about."

"Is that why Jonathan wasn't at the hospital? Wait, is that why he left on this big trip?"

"That's why. He felt very strongly that I should have told you, and that I should have told him, too. While I understand where he's coming from, we see things differently."

"Too differently?"

"Apparently, yes."

Becca blew out a long breath. "This is a lot to get my head around."

"It is, sweetie. I'm so . . ." Silence, as once again the person on the other end of the line hung up.

AFTER MEETING with the director Monday morning and lining up houses to look at for the show, he spent the rest of the week driving up and down Highway One, from Dana Point to Malibu. The last place he toured near Laguna

Beach was a real stunner, a $50 million glass-walled mansion—with a dining room table for eighteen—sited high on a craggy cliff above a secluded cove. A sedate but sexy party house, perfect for the show's well heeled, over forty-five, wish-I-had-a-$50-million beach house demographic.

After touring the house, he stopped at a coffee shop in town to take a quick break and type up some notes. He hadn't gotten far when his phone thrummed against the table.

Not again. Was Quinn trying to mess with him, or what? She kept sending him these texts, like small diary entries, little poems that didn't rhyme but still sounded lyrical. Not that he read poetry, but if he did, this is probably what it would sound like.

Except he was pretty sure it wouldn't make him angry and a cocktail of other feelings he couldn't even put his finger on—and that reading her words wouldn't make him hard.

He actually had gotten an erection the other day. From one of her texts. It wasn't the messages themselves; it was picturing her composing them, picturing her fingers as she typed, imagining her voice saying the words.

He hadn't answered because he needed more time to think this shit-storm through. And his thinking wasn't so clear with wood in his pants.

In the past, in his single days, if that flight attendant had propositioned him, the primal, reptilian part of his brain would have gone for it. He would have slipped through that literal and figurative doorway in a flash.

But not now. Not after Quinn. Even exasperated and stung by her decisions, the idea of sleeping with another woman—Delphine in Paris, the flight attendant—it did nothing for him.

Nuh-*thing*. Not a twitch of arousal.

Unlike the damn texts that forced him to step behind the nearest piece of waist-high furniture or adjust his napkin until his dick chilled.

He had seen little of that flight attendant for the rest of the trip. Another member of the crew had poured him water and brought him a third, or fourth, vodka. Maybe she was miffed he hadn't looked for her in the staff quarters. Maybe she was assigned to a different cabin after her break, who knew.

But then on his way off the plane, he caught a glimpse of her standing in the other aisle, controlling the flow of passengers merging into one line toward the exit to the jet bridge.

Rather, he caught a glimpse of her thin gold wedding band.

He was certain she hadn't been wearing one earlier, and he imagined her taking it out of her pocket, sliding it back on right before landing. Before her husband, or wife, pulled up to the curb outside baggage claim, possibly with kids in the backseat. Before she returned to her real, on-the-ground life.

He made no attempt to catch her eye as he left the plane. He was the last person to judge—he had been no saint when he was married—but the thought that had popped into his head at that moment was a simple one.

Quinn would never do that.

She might have made a mistake or exercised what from his vantage point was extremely crappy judgment, or he might not be able to accept her allegiances, but she would not cheat.

And that had led him over the past few days to a small but not insignificant kernel of truth: He could choose to be with her or he could choose to live without her, but she was not going to change. Maybe it was the damn poetic notes she kept sending him, but now he was no longer sure he wanted her to.

————

BY THE END of the week, she had written to the end of the second notebook and started on the third. It might be dumb to believe it was the notebooks themselves that inspired her, but she was superstitious that way. In the past, she had only used those marbled black and white ones. From now on, she would only write in the notebooks she bought in Paris.

At the speed she was working, she would need to restock soon. Maybe she could find that little shop online and ask them to ship her an order.

Today, she wrote through lunch and the late afternoon, the setting sun and pink cast of the sky alerting her it was time to take a break to eat something.

And make another phone call.

After she washed her plate and utensils, she picked up her phone. Still without looking for a text from Jonathan that wouldn't be there, she called Leigh.

"Are you free for lunch this week?" Quinn asked, after Leigh updated her on Becca's condition.

"Why don't we meet at Becca and Charles's apartment, since she's home? I'll order lunch to be delivered." Clearly, Becca hadn't told her.

"Actually, I could use some one-on-one time with you."

They agreed on coffee the next morning before Leigh went to visit Becca.

At the bustling cafe, they ordered lattes—Leigh's skinny

as always; Quinn's with whole milk—and dashed toward two club chairs in a quiet corner the second the occupants stood up to leave.

The way Leigh was talking about Becca, Quinn could tell she did not know what was really going on with her daughter.

Finally Leigh said, "So, dish. One-on-one time to tell me . . ." She looked at Quinn coyly. "Are you and Jonathan . . . Do you have news?" She held up and wiggled her ring finger.

Quinn set down her mug so she wouldn't spill it. "Not that kind of news, I'm afraid." Her lips were so tense, her attempt to smile must seem like a nervous tic.

"A lot's happened since Harris. And since the night you arranged that dinner. A lot has changed in my life."

Leigh continued to look hopeful. "Jonathan."

"Yes, Jonathan, for one. He was a wonderful surprise." She would not say that they were separated right now. As much as she wanted him back in her life, at the moment that fact was irrelevant.

"Do you remember—you and I had lunch a few weeks back, and you mentioned a submission from a debut erotica writer? And you hated it."

"Unfortunately, I remember," she said drolly, swiping a hand down each arm. *Ick, get it off me.*

"The things in those pages? The protagonist's discovery of that lifestyle? I experienced that, that's why I wrote about it. I wrote those pages, and I sent them to you under a pen name."

Leigh's face contorted. She looked as though she were listening to Quinn speak a foreign language and her dictionary was missing key words.

"It's a part of my life now—those things, and writing about them. I shared those pages with you, hoping you would have liked the writing and the approach and at least been open, curious, about the material. I shouldn't have expected you to understand, but your reaction, it . . . well, it really disappointed me."

This was an understatement. "I felt embarrassed, ashamed even. So I kept the truth from you. But now, I'm owning it. That was my work. Inspired by my experience here in New York and in Paris. I lied to you about that trip I took right before the wedding—I wasn't in Paris to shop with an old friend. You should know the truth. I'm sorry I lied to you."

She couldn't quite read Leigh's expression now, but it wasn't shock. "You looked so crestfallen when I said I hated —I didn't like—those pages that the thought did cross my mind. And then I remembered I'd heard some mumblings among some other authors that you had been spotted at . . . at that famous dungeon, Ophelia's."

"Octavia's."

"But frankly, I put it out of my mind. I wasn't going to represent that kind of work, and unless you confronted me with it directly, I didn't really want to think about it. If we're going to be honest and confessional here, I found the . . . lifestyle, as you call it, in that story unrelatable. And that it was based on events you experienced, well that's a little too much information even between the two of us. I don't want to hear, or read, every graphic detail of your private life, no matter how well written."

Funny, but wasn't it Leigh who doggedly asked for details of her relationship with Jonathan? Wasn't it Leigh who had encouraged her to "move on" and stop grieving on day three hundred sixty six after Harris died? It had been

Quinn who kept the details light, not wanting to say too much until she and Jonathan found their footing.

". . . the sting of a slender cane on one's backside? Really, Quinn. That was unnecessary, and heavy-handed."

Pun definitely not intended.

Quinn would not let Leigh take this away from her. This was Leigh's problem, not hers. And the lifestyle Leigh disparaged existed a lot closer to her own small world than she realized. Would she say these same things to the son-in-law she was gaga over—or to her own daughter, if Becca decided to join him?

With Leigh's attitude, the secrets would never end.

"I would encourage you," Leigh was saying now, "to think long and hard about your reputation before you send out more pages to anyone else, if you're considering doing that. Don't sabotage your career. I don't understand why you can't go back to writing literature. You're an award-winning author, for goodness' sake. Last time we talked about your professional life, I was trying to convince you to re-apply to Hollinger. Do you think that smut—I'm sorry if that hurts your feelings, but that's how I categorize it—is going to get you another shot at a fellowship?"

Unbelievable. "That's what this is all about—you're worried about my reputation?"

"One of us ought to be," Leigh shot back. "Your *reputation* is everything, Quinn. Your *reputation* is what's made it possible not to get sued by your publisher for not delivering your last book. It's me who's been keeping their lawyers at bay pulling the but-she's-been-through-a-tragedy card while you've been jetting off to get tied up and spanked. Your *reputation* is what's going to make it possible to get over the career slump that, quite frankly, has gone on way too long. I've invested a lot in you and, more than that, I helped you get out of your pajamas and off your couch and back among the liv . . . back among society. I wish you would appreciate that investment more—I wish you could appreciate that I want you to succeed."

Leigh sat back, crossed her arms, and added the pièce de résistance: "And really, Quinn, I don't see how writing that trash is going to accomplish that."

Now Quinn's dictionary was the one missing words. She couldn't believe what she was hearing. What had happened in Leigh's past to turn her to stone?

"Let's get something straight," Quinn mustered, her fists clenched beside her thighs. "I don't *owe* you anything. You made a lot of money, for *years*, from my creativity, from my hard work. So we are more than square on that. As for my *reputation* and deliverables, if Devon Publishing has any questions about either, you can tell Nely to call me directly since you no longer represent me."

She leaned forward to pick up her bag from the floor beside her chair. "The very sad truth," she said, as she straightened up, "is that it took Harris dying for me to realize how removed you can be from emotion. You know, feelings?" She exaggerated the question. "We humans experience them every now and then. Especially between friends, although you've been pretty shitty at that the last year and a half also."

———

THE MELLOW CAFE by the Malibu Pier had become his favorite work hangout—the saltwater air, the sound of the surf, the faint smell of weed wafting by every once in a while, the funny bits of conversation—mostly from the tourists but not only. This was California, and he had to admit, he could picture himself spending more time here. The chill vibe, the weather, the anonymity—no one gave him a second glance here since there were way more interesting and recognizable personalities all around.

And way fewer memories.

He pushed his empty breakfast plate to the side of the table and went back to the open documents on his laptop screen.

A wave crashed against the pilings beneath the pier, almost drowning out the sound of his phone chirping with a text. He turned it over. Quinn again. He shifted the napkin in his lap for optimal coverage, anticipating the effect.

> Morning. How's California today? I talked to Becca. And Leigh. You won't be surprised—neither went very well. You still won't answer; I still miss you.

This one didn't possess quite the same lyricism. She was upset, he could tell, and despite him still being pissed off and his feelings still bruised, the tenor of her message made him want to go to her. He would wrap his arms around her and whisper that everything would be okay and kiss her cheek lightly and hold her head and . . . he was in a public place and so he would not think about how she smelled, especially her hair.

Not only did this particular text engage his dick; it also punched right through his chest, casting off whatever anger remained there.

Although he shouldn't pick on that flight attendant, he kept envisioning the wedding band on her finger. It was possible she and her spouse had an agreement, an understanding—what happens in the air stays in the air—or an open marriage. But, whatever. Point being, he didn't have to look far to see examples of people who had made a mistake, done the wrong thing.

He could, for instance, look in the mirror.

Don't be so self-righteous.

He had told Quinn many times how important honesty and intimacy were to him now after what he had done to Delphine, and he had gotten both in spades with her. She bared herself to him like no one had before, and they shared a level of closeness he hadn't even had with the woman he married.

Quinn was strong. She was thoughtful. She would go to the mat for people, for principles. That this issue stood between them was evidence of that. Maybe she hadn't done the wrong thing after all.

Or maybe she should have told him, chosen loyalty to him over loyalty to Octavia's and the other members. Maybe she should have told Becca—Charles, his double life at the club, and the rest of the community be damned.

He shifted uncomfortably in his seat, suddenly restless. If he were honest, that alternate path didn't feel right either.

His phone buzzed again. *Not another one.* He would need to go back to the bungalow and take a cold shower if she kept texting. It was ridiculous, this inexplicable physical response to her words, to her.

It was still buzzing—with a call, not a text. He turned the screen over as Becca's name scrolled across. "Hey you!" he answered. "How are you feeling?"

"Big, heavy, and stir crazy. But it's all good." She sounded tired. "What's this I hear about you and California?"

"It's true. I'm in California. Malib . . ."

"Doing what exactly?"

"Working on a project with an old colleague. I . . ."

"Ran away."

Another wave crashed; maybe he hadn't heard her right. "What'd you say?"

"You ran away. Charles told me you canceled the deal. He told me a lot more, but let's not go there just yet. He's a great businessperson, with good instincts so you can't do better than him. And he wouldn't have agreed to invest our money if he didn't believe your idea, your plans, would be super-successful. So you're good for him, for us, too."

Our money. Us. A good sign, but still.

"If you want to talk about why I backed out, we'll need to talk about the rest." As he said it, his chest sunk—the more his indignation faded, the less he liked how he sounded.

"Okay, Jonathan. First, I know you're trying to look out for me, but I'm a grownup . . ." He smiled at her deliberate upward lilt at the end of the word, which made her sound anything but fully adult.

But, point taken.

". . . and I don't need you fighting my battles. Charles had his reasons for not telling me. We started to see a therapist, and I'm beginning to understand. Some days I want to leave him, like when I think about how often he must have lied to me. But—I know this sounds crazy—I know he really loves me, and I love him. I can't just give that up, you know? Especially now that we're going to be parents. Together or apart, we need to figure this out. *We* being Charles and me —no one else."

She cleared her throat and waited for him to respond.

"Okay, I hear you. I understand what you're saying."

"Good. So butt out."

He chuckled. "I'm out, I'm out." Even with this on her shoulders, she was funny and tough.

"So, moving on to you . . ."

"Must we?" he asked sardonically.

"We must. Quinn shared some of your issues with me—how she discovered this thing about herself and you two worked out a way that she could be part of it and not violate the boundaries of your relationship. You guys are my model now, so you can't break up."

"I'm not sure about the boundaries part." As he spoke, he gazed down the pier at the surfers.

"Jonathan, I was angry with her at first too, but she was caught in a really impossible situation. She did right by Charles and, honestly, if she—or you—*had* come to me, I'm not sure I would have believed either of you. Or I would have gotten totally defensive because how shitty would it be for a third party to tell you about some big ol' issue in your new marriage you had no freaking idea about."

She raised good points, but he kept quiet because she was not stopping.

"But no matter what happens, if Charles and I get through this or we split up, Quinn had nothing to do with it. If anything, she pushed me to consider possibilities for our relationship I never would have. Maybe I'll get into it too, who knows?"

"Okay, moving into too-much-information territory," he joked. But he, too, had been changed by Quinn. In the best way. He was the professional traveler, the expert on—hah!—people and places. And yet she had opened his eyes to a new world.

"Yeah, sorry. Hormones. Stress. Therapy. I'm an open book. So back to you again. You sought Charles out as an investor, and he wanted to back your business plan. Let him. Take the money, use him as an advisor, start your company. And you're in love with Quinn."

She paused. He stayed silent, and she went on. "So why are you in California?"

He laughed and opened his mouth to speak, although he still wasn't sure what he was going to say.

"Shh. Not finished. If she told you about Charles, or you told me, it wouldn't have changed anything. It wouldn't have helped, and I wouldn't be thinking you were some kind of hero for bringing it to my attention. What I'm saying is, Quinn did the right thing. I want more friends like her."

"You're right, kiddo," he said. "I do, too."

17

DECISIONS

She hurried through the wooden doors and into the Grand Central Terminal foyer, as if physically getting away from Leigh could diminish the impact of what she had just said.

As she fed her credit card into the ticket machine, she noticed tiny arches across her palm, nail imprints from clenched fists. Her jaw was also clenched, and she relaxed that too.

She hadn't expected Leigh to embrace her disclosure, but she did not expect that much judgment. Or the comments about her career. *Tell me what you really think.* Or the contempt. It felt terrible. She understood why Octavia kept her distance from people, tried not to get attached. And why Charles kept that part of his life hidden. Even to his wife. To see such disdain reflected in the face of someone you confided in, who you believed knew you? It hurt. A lot.

Even Jonathan had looked at her that way in the car on the way to the airport, for the brief few seconds he actually did look at her.

As the train rattled through the tunnel and north along the river, she looked on her phone at his social media accounts. He had posted a few photos of meals by the water, a beach with a bunch of surfers—Malibu?—funky building facades, a pod of dolphins in the Pacific set against a bright sky.

Maybe he wouldn't come back to New York after this trip. Maybe he wouldn't come back to her.

But still, she hoped. Her car ambush had been an ill-conceived disaster. She wished there was some other way to show him how she felt about him, about them.

But as the days went by and he didn't respond to her texts, hope waned.

When the train arrived at her station, she bypassed the line of waiting taxis and walked to the farmhouse; she needed the movement and the cool air.

By the time she put her key in the front door lock, she had made several decisions.

She would not stop writing. What she had sent to Leigh a few weeks ago, "the smut," she would turn into a couple of short fictional stories. Their names, she already had come up with on the walk home.

This new manuscript that Quinn had been working on —she suddenly realized how she could show Jonathan how she felt. She would focus all her energy on it and finish it as quickly as she could, because it was for two—no, three— incredibly important reasons: herself, him, and their future. This was how she could show him what he meant to her, and—she desperately hoped—help him find a way back to her.

She dropped her purse by the table in the front hall and threw her coat over the stair railing. In the kitchen, she made a cup of tea. Other than the trip to Paris with Octavia for Madame's celebration, which hadn't been scheduled yet, she would continue to spend a lot of time here.

Not at Jonathan's. Not at the club. Here. Home. Writing.

Finishing.

Carefully, she carried the mug upstairs to her office. This would be her routine. Every day. A morning walk, a cup of tea, filling her notebooks with the rest of the story.

She took the top notebook off the pile on her desk and turned to where she left off yesterday.

That's the routine she stuck to, day after day. Breaking only for the essentials and her rewards for especially good writing days—a candle-lit evening bath or a dinner with Octavia.

When writing the steamy scenes, she would think of how Jonathan touched her. She would make herself come, his effect on her still so strong, even in his absence. She missed him sharply in those moments; those climaxes, like much of their relationship, were bittersweet.

And every day, she took a long walk—through town, down to the river, in the woods after the first snowfall, each day a different route to discover something new, something she could tell him about someday.

She kept on sending him the texts. As with the manuscript, she would not let her determination wane. He had stood by her in her worst moments, and she would do the same while he worked through his anger and hurt.

The hurt she caused because she hid something from him. But she also knew the roots of that wound ran deeper and further back in time than the two of them. The ghosts of his past, his regrets, his needs borne of past failures—would they ever fully fade away? She had her own, that's for sure, and she understood his need for time, but she also knew its preciousness; she would not waste any.

Yesterday, she had finally run out of the notebooks from Paris, so she took an old black and white marbled one from her desk drawer to start the last scene this morning. The real story was not over, but the manuscript was reaching its natural conclusion—for now.

When she finished, she placed her pen on the desk, sat back in her chair, and let that satisfying feeling of completion, of accomplishment, fill her. It was a rough first draft, very rough; she was far from done. But now she had pages to work with, a story to shape and to be shaped by.

She had written many books, but this story in particular —its characters, its events, its subtle as well as life-altering twists—molded the author as much as she, it.

Later, she would call Nely at Devon and ask for a meeting to talk about the future.

She would send pages to Hollinger to see about a new fellowship; she might even send the committee those erotic pages she had shared with Leigh.

And one day, after more time passed and her heart wouldn't ache so deeply, she would write another story, about the past, about Harris.

After a while, she picked up the pen again for one last thing. She always saved writing her dedications until the end, and that's where she liked to put them in her books, on the very last page.

The clean white leaf of paper was cool against the heel of her hand as she wrote. There was no need to think about what this one would say.

18

UNFINISHED

J onathan lay in bed, apparently done sleeping for the
night even though the sun had yet to raise a bleary
eyebrow over the horizon. The question Becca voiced
on the phone surfaced in his brain, the question he had
been pussyfooting around asking himself, *Why are you in
California?*

It was becoming a good question. He needed to finish
this gig—shooting at the glass house on the cliff had a couple
more weeks to go—but then what?

Quinn was smart, compassionate, and kind, and he
knew, since her discovery about Charles and all its fallout,
broken-hearted. He heard that in her texts, the sadness, but
also he heard her doggedness, her hope, her faith in the two
of them. Yesterday, she texted him a single photo of delicate
bird tracks in the lightest dusting of snow on her deck rail,
tiny little footprints.

What's it like where you are?

When he first left New York, he told himself they were

over as a couple. But as the days turned into weeks, he knew Becca was right—he had run away. Because he was angry. Because he felt betrayed. And maybe also because falling—being—in love was scary, the risks of having your heart crushed omnipresent.

Quinn was strong and principled. If he were half the person she was, he wouldn't have cheated. But her strength, those principles, also meant that if something like what happened with Charles were to arise again, she probably would make the same decision—she would not tell Jonathan everything. He would have to be okay with that.

Could he be?

He let the fantasy reel play in his mind. If he were in New York right now, he would pack a lunch and a heavy blanket and get on the next train to see her so they could talk. They would huddle under the blanket and look out together at the river, the edges beginning to freeze, ducks gliding in the warmer pockets, as they shared the food. Or if it was too windy, they would sit inside, in front of her fireplace. They would talk, guarded at first, but soon laughing softly, each of them reopening to the other.

When they finished eating, he would follow her upstairs. They'd make love, mess up the sheets in her sunny, white room, clothes strewn all around. When they finally got up sometime, oh, late in the afternoon, he would look in her mostly empty fridge, find a few eggs and whip them up for dinner so they wouldn't have to put on real clothes and go out.

But that was a daydream. While his lizard brain and other parts wanted to mess up her sheets, the rest of him was well aware of the reality. Like she told him before, their relationship was what sparked her interest in the lifestyle. He could share it with her, including accepting that there would be secrets she might not be able to tell him, or he could let her go.

Although he didn't have to meet the cast and crew at the house until seven thirty, he showered and grabbed his stuff for the day and left the bungalow early. The park near the glass house was a perfect place to catch the sunrise.

He knew the exact image he wanted to capture: the bluff with a single cypress in silhouette against the glowing golden-violet dawn light. He framed it with the Pacific in the foreground, reflecting the color burst in the sky.

The image was fierce and stark at the same time.

Hot-headed and lonely.

He opened a new text message and sent the picture. Just the picture. Her medium was words; he was better with images.

It was after nine in New York, so she was probably awake. Making coffee, or showering, which he would not think about. But then the three sequential bubbles darkened and faded a few times and he pictured her typing and deleting, second-guessing herself after his long silence. She had told him she loved him on that horrific ride to the airport. After what she had been through with Harris, acknowledging that, saying those words to another man, could not have been easy.

And how had Jonathan responded? He had been a cold son of a bitch. Got out of the car. Turned his back. Walked away. Then ignored her.

The bubbles stopped, but no text popped up.

What did you expect, a brass band? A red fucking carpet?

He put the phone back in his pocket, found a place to grab breakfast, and got his brain focused on the scenes they would shoot today.

By the time early evening rolled around, they had two scenes in the can and a third blocked so they could start shooting early tomorrow. They didn't get as far as he planned today, but they had done respectable work. Bryan was right. They were a good bunch. The jokes passed easily among them, at least most of the time; they shared a real sense of camaraderie.

In fact, they were going out for drinks and dinner in Laguna Beach now, but he begged off, wanting to charge his dead phone.

When he got back to Bryan's guest house, there was a thick envelope propped against the frame of the front door.

He recognized the handwriting immediately. For a second, he wondered how she found him here, but then he remembered a text from Becca asking questions about where he was staying. He hoped she was a co-conspirator in tracking him down; if that were the case, it meant she and Quinn were on speaking terms.

Inside the bungalow, he opened the envelope and slid out the stack of pages, bound in the upper left corner with a black metal clip. There was no note, only a blank cover sheet followed by pages and pages of handwriting, text scanned from a notebook. The notebooks she had showed him from Paris, he guessed.

Her tenacity brought a smile to his face. She had said she was writing again, but this, this was a lot of words. The scanning alone must have taken her half a day.

He turned to the first page as he sat on the bed and began to read.

At some point, he got up to close the blinds and order a burger to be delivered. Then he went back to reading.

He remembered opening the door and tipping the guy

who brought the food, but he hardly recalled now how it tasted; he had gotten so lost in her words.

Sometime after two a.m., he brushed his teeth, turned off the overhead light, and flicked on the small reading lamp on the nightstand. He dropped his clothes on the floor by the side of the bed and got in to finish the last few pages.

It was their story, in three parts. She had written their brief history. Quiet and melancholy at the start, slowly transforming into something warmer—passionate and layered.

The frame in his mind filled with detail—colors and sounds, textures and scents. The white lace of her lingerie, the smokey chocolate he had savored on her skin. The cool limestone buildings and the fire of Paris. Blues, greens, and grays of the ocean near her old house and the river near her new one, the warm glow of the lanterns in the barn at the wedding.

The feelings, the discoveries, the sensuality—she had created a narrative scrapbook of the extraordinary time they shared, of the relationship they had started to build.

How she felt about him throughout their evolution, what she was afraid of, how she observed and knew him—it was all there in black and white, in the weight of the pages he held in his hands.

She had written about the woman she was that first night, grieving and broken, aching to be touched but disgusted by her desire. She had written about the man who had understood her on a plane beyond words, who had slowly, silently, turned cold, anguished distance into warmth and healing, pleasure and love.

She wrote about the club and Paris, about exploration and pain, about secrets and loyalties and trust. One particular paragraph near the end rang leaden in his chest:

She needed an epiphany. She kept thinking about how they could be together, what their resolution could be. She wanted one so much. But it wasn't coming. Maybe that was the epiphany, that there was no good solution. Maybe it was more this quiet knowing and acceptance despite the costs, rather than discovery. That didn't mean it wasn't breaking her heart—or that she couldn't still fight for the man she loved.

Only how do you fight for someone and also tell them, if I had to do it over I would make the same choice, I might hurt you like this again.

It was heartbreaking to admit because she knew what it meant for them.

Only she was wrong.

He would not want her to make a different choice, or to give up the lifestyle that had helped her face her grief, that had taken them to such depths of pleasure and intimacy. It was all part of what they shared. It was rare and special, this kind of connection that, until Quinn, he had been too chicken-shit fearful to embrace.

If they were to have a future together, he would have to trust her unconditionally. Other things might happen at the club that she wouldn't be able to share with him, and he would have to trust her actions, her decisions, her principles. Her love.

And his for her. He was crazy about this beautiful, talented woman whose way of living reminded him of the man he strived to be.

She made him laugh, too. The bit she made up about him counting backwards so he wouldn't come too fast? That was funny. Although it was wrong. He didn't count; in real life, he had spelled. The names of countries he hadn't been to yet. It took more focus than counting, which for his purposes made it more effective.

There were other gaps, but he could help her fill in the details later. Before publication. Because he knew this story would become a book. And with his production company, the one he was going to start, he could work with her to adapt it for the screen. Maybe, if Charles forgave him, he also would be involved.

When Jonathan turned the last page and read her dedication, his decision to commit to her, his complete and utter certainty he could trust as deeply as she needed him to, crystalized.

He got out of bed and took his laptop from the desk by the window. The airline website showed a couple of seats still left on the red eye scheduled to depart later today. He could only spend one day in New York, but he had to see her. The crew could shoot tomorrow without him—he would make sure everything was all set before he left tonight.

He clicked to make a reservation, then started a new text. It was barely sunrise by her, but he willed her to be awake.

Hi.

The three dots told him she was.

Hi.

Thank you for the manuscript. It's wonderful

. . .

But the story feels unfinished to me.

I hope it's not finished.

What are you doing tomorrow morning?
I'm planning to come to NY.

What I've been doing every day since you
left. Writing.

Can you take a few hours off? My flight
arrives at seven a.m. I'll see if Gil can pick
you up. Meet me at JFK?

Layover?

No. You. I need to see you.

Did you read the whole thing, to the end? I
don't want to get my hopes up, or you to
waste a trip.

I read every word. That is exactly why I'm
coming to see you.

A big-smile emoji popped up on his screen.

I'll make us breakfast.

He started to type that she shouldn't bother, because in
the few hours they would have together, he was not planning to waste time eating breakfast.

But he deleted it.

Can I still tell you to wear that black skirt?

Octavia's back, so I've been off duty.

But I liked our arrangement.

I did too.

Good. In that case, black skirt

. . .

and no panties.

Yes, Jonathan. Yes.

HE PUT the manuscript on the desk beside his laptop and set his phone alarm to allow a couple-of-hour nap before meeting the cast and crew. It wasn't enough sleep, but coffee and adrenaline would carry him through. He would rest on the plane tonight.

When the phone alarm went off, he showered, threw a change of clothes into his bag, and composed a sheepish, awkward text to Charles, asking if he would have a few minutes to talk tomorrow.

Apologizing to Charles face to face while he was in New York would be the one and only time he planned to leave Quinn's side. Well, that and a visit to a jeweler.

He would not blindside her with a proposal just yet, but her manuscript—it told him everything he needed to know, and he wanted to give her something precious in return to symbolize his commitment and intention.

Now, he thought, maybe a collar.

The future might not work out exactly as he wanted, as he was setting his heart on—a new business venture with Charles as a major investor and, more importantly, his life with Quinn—but he had to take the risk. And no, he no longer needed to look at the word *dare* tattooed on his wrist to remind him.

It was time to head to the glass house. He packed up his laptop and picked up the manuscript. Before slipping it into his bag, he flipped once more to the last page. Her dedication—he had memorized it but, still, he wanted to read it again; he would never grow tired of her words.

For Jonathan
Our story began only recently, but already I am yours.
Entirely.

THANK YOU FOR READING *ENTIRELY!* Please consider leaving a review on your preferred retailer and book review sites—or tell a friend about it.

Want news about new books and advance review copy access? Feel free to add your email to my list.

You can access bonus Reader & Book Club Guides for *Silently*, *Secretly*, and *Entirely* at my website, talyablaine.com.

Thank you again. Your support means the world.

Turn the page for an Author's Note about *Entirely*.

AUTHOR'S NOTE

Thank you for reading *Entirely*. I hope you loved the book. From the writing perspective, it was quite a wild ride. As with the first two books in the Transformation series, I let the characters lead. I love how Jonathan gets the idea for public play and it really (clears throat) works for each of them individually and as a couple, with the interplay of intimacy and potential exposure as well as protection, control, and trust. I also love how he rises to the challenge of being more dominant with Quinn while she manages the club, although he's not so comfy with either of their roles.

Early on in their relationship, and even more strongly in this book, Jonathan realizes he has to get used to how Quinn needs him. But somehow—because of how in love he is with her, I would say—this helps him come to trust and believe in himself again. None of it is easy for him, including the awareness that he wouldn't be with Quinn had Harris not died. Which plays smack dab into his feeling undeserving of the good things that have happened in his life.

He keeps challenging himself, though, and it was hard

to write the second half of *Entirely* once I knew that he would feel so utterly betrayed.

But love triumphs—this is a romance, after all—and he's adorable at the end when he asks in one of his texts if he can still tell her what to wear. It's one of my favorite lines of his because it shows in just a few words his sexiness, sense of humor, and sweetness.

Unquenchable chemistry, these two. I'm curious what their future holds.

XO,
Talya

ABOUT THE AUTHOR

A late-blooming romance reader and romance writer, Talya Blaine writes older characters, including strong heroines and sexy beta heroes, and in exploring how relationships change with time.

When she's not working at her day job in marketing, she loves to write, read, and blog about steamy romances; hike with her border collie; and spend time with Mr. Blaine, her real-life romance hero.

Learn more at talyablaine.com.

ALSO BY TALYA BLAINE

Transformation Series

Silently (Book 1)

"This is a unique work with fascinating characters, drawn together as they individually recover from profound loss." -The BookLife Prize

Secretly (**Book 2**)

"Blaine excels at crafting a plausible plot and ratcheting up the heat and chemistry..."

"Hot and deliciously steamy..." -The BookLife Prize

Entirely (**Book 3**)

"Blaine continues the Transformation series with this third installment, spilling over with steamy bedroom scenes..."

"...the deep interplay between the two main characters adds a special intimacy to the novel." -The BookLife Prize